FINDING MERCY

THE NEXT GENERATION
BOOK 3

RILEY EDWARDS

BE A REBEL

Finding Mercy
The Next Generation

Cover design: Jena Brignola

Written by: Riley Edwards

Published by: Riley Edwards/Rebels Romance

Edited by: Eve Arroyo

Proofreader: Kendall Barnett

Finding Mercy

SPECIAL EDITION

Paperback ISBN: 978-1-951567-35-4

First edition: **December 26, 2022**

To my family - my team – my tribe.
This is for you.

CONTENTS

FINDING MERCY AUDIO

Performed By: Troy Duran & Devon Grace

PROLOGUE

"IT'S TIME, JAY."

Panic rose at Kayla's words, and the lump in my throat threatened to choke me. I couldn't swallow past the fear. Selfishly, I wasn't ready. The finality of the situation was more than I could comprehend.

"Just . . ." I didn't know what I was trying to say.

Just hold on?

Just let go?

"You've given up enough for me. It's time to let me go."

"Don't say that, Kayla. You know I'd give up everything if I could save you."

"And you have. You've given up the last seven years of your life taking care of me. It's time for you to move on. Live. Be happy. Find someone to love."

Love? What the hell did I know about love? I didn't know the first thing about loving someone. I'd failed in every way possible. My wife's frail body in my arms was proof. She'd wasted away right in front of me. I'd help-lessly watched as cancer had ravished her body. Stolen years from her. Love? Yeah, fuck love.

"Kayla."

"Promise me, Jason. You'll never know how grateful I am that you've stuck by me. Because of you, I had seven extra years. I'm just sorry it was at your expense."

"I love you, Kayla. I don't regret anything."

What I felt for Kayla was as close to love as I'd ever feel.

"I love you, too, Jason." Her voice was starting to fade.

"I'm right here, Kay Kay. I won't leave your side." I couldn't stop the tears as they streamed down my cheeks. "It's okay to let go. I promise everything will be okay."

"Thank you, Jay." She sounded sleepy, her voice raspy. "Love . . ."

"I love you, too."

Sweat beaded on my forehead as I jolted awake in a cold and empty bed.

I'd lied to Kayla in her final moments of her life. I'd promised her everything would be okay, but it wasn't.

Every night I've dreamt of that promise, reliving the worst day of my life over and over again. It was what I deserved.

A husband barely out of high school and a widower by twenty-eight—ain't life grand?

Not bothering to straighten the crumpled comforter, I headed to the shower to scrub away the lingering effects of my dream. The sweat and tears were easy to wash down the drain. The guilt and regret were etched so deep nothing would ever clean the stains away.

With my skin damn near raw from my shower, I went through the motions of starting my day. I was like a fucking robot. I was numb. So many times I'd considered selling the house but I couldn't. I was trapped behind the wood and bricks. Locked inside with Kayla's ghost.

Remembering I had to grab files from my home office, I darted into the room to grab them before I headed to work. I picked up the envelope with the documents I needed, and my heart constricted.

A separation agreement sat on the desktop taunting me, reminding me, mocking the memory of my wife. Kayla's pretty handwriting flowing across the page. She'd signed it. This stupid fucking piece of paper was supposed to be her way out. She was supposed to finally find happiness. Get her happily ever after. The one she could never find with me.

I was a shit husband. A shit human being.

No. Nothing was ever going to be okay again.

1

"WHAT HAS YOU SO PISSED OFF?" Special Agent Mercy James asked when she stopped in front of my desk.

"Nothing." I tried to hide my irritation.

"Doesn't look like nothing to me the way you're pounding on your keyboard."

I knew she was trying to lighten the atmosphere, but I wasn't in the mood. I hated this month. The day was fast approaching, and I hated that, too. Two years. Two shitty years since I'd last seen Kayla. Two years since I'd held her in my arms and she'd drawn her last breath. No, I wasn't in the mood to joke around about why I was abusing my keyboard.

Before I could close the email, Mercy saw it. The yearly cancer survivor benefit. Only, the person who had indeed survived cancer once had lost the second battle. Someone needed to update their goddamn files. That was what I was in the middle of doing when Mercy disrupted me. I was drafting a strongly worded email about their record keeping.

"Sorry." Mercy softened her voice, and that pissed me off more than her trying to be funny. I'd worked with her for a long time. She and all the other DEA agents knew about my dead wife. They'd all had a front row seat to my grief.

"Why are you sorry?"

She didn't deserve my attitude. I was being a dick and I knew it. Mercy meant well, but, damn, enough already. I was tired of the I'm sorrys and empty platitudes. No one knew what to say to someone who'd lost a loved one, because there was nothing to say. It was what it was. Death was final. Nothing makes the ache and pain vanish. It flat out fucking sucked, and there was nothing else to say but that.

"Damn, Mercy, I'm being an asshole. Sorry about that. The anniversary of Kayla's death is next week, and I'm on edge and taking it out on you. I hope you can forgive me."

Her brows drew together, and a familiar look of pain crossed her face before she masked it. The old Jason would've inquired. But the new fucked-up Jason was happy when she smiled and brushed my douchebaggery away.

"I get it."

By her previous look I'd say she did, but, again, I ignored the look and the pang of remorse for not asking if she was okay.

"What brings you down here?" I asked, changing the subject.

Mercy worked upstairs as a diversion investigator. The diversion control department dealt with legitimate pharmaceuticals that made their way to the streets for illicit use. She'd transferred down to Georgia from Virginia about five years ago. She was one of the best in her division.

"I wanted to ask your opinion on the Polytech High School case. I left the report on your desk a few days ago."

I grabbed the manila folder off my desk and handed it to her, she sat in one of the two chairs in my office and opened the file.

"I agree with the local PD, they have a problem and would benefit from a narc being put in place," I answered.

"I'd like you to work with me on the case."

"Why?" The question slipped out before I could stop it. It wasn't unusual for my task force to work with the diversion team, but my team mainly stuck to the trafficking and transportation of narcotics.

"Two reasons. One because I need someone with your instincts, and two, because I think this goes beyond a bunch of kids stealing their parents' prescription meds and selling them to their friends."

"You think one of the parents is in on it?"

"I'm not sure what I think, but with two overdoses in six months, three more hospitalizations, and five from the surrounding schools, all with the same chemical makeup, tells me this is spreading. That means I need all the help I can get."

I sat back in my chair and studied Mercy. This should've been a no brainer for me. High school kids were passing around benzos like they were Tic Tacs. I joined the DEA to save lives, especially those most vulnerable. Something I couldn't put my finger on was nagging the back of my mind, telling me to stay far away from this case. Or was it Mercy and her pretty smile I needed to stay away from?

"Tell me when we're starting and I'll be there."

As soon as the words left my mouth, and Mercy's lips tipped up, I had my answer. It wasn't the case that had all the fine hairs on the back of my neck standing, it was her. She was dangerous.

She stood and reached her hand over my desk. I was trying to ignore how her small hand fit in mine when she took mine in a firm grip and shook. I was really trying to overlook the way her soft skin felt against mine. But the thing I was most trying to evade was the fact that I was feeling anything at all.

"Great. I'll see you this afternoon."

I even watched as she left my office.

2

WHEN I WAS a kid my dad used to tell me that one day my lack of self-preservation was going to get me into trouble. When I was ten, he was talking about me learning how to do wheelies on my bicycle. When I was sixteen, he was talking about me jumping off the roof of our house into the pool below. And when I was twenty, it was because I'd decided to go into law enforcement.

However, if he were alive, I think this would be the time he'd say, you've gone too far. This torture I was putting myself through had nothing to do with my need for an adrenaline rush. Or me being a daredevil. No, I'd been tormenting myself over the last three months by working with Jason Walker. It had started the day I'd asked him to join my team and investigate pharmaceuticals and other drugs running through some of our local schools. Over the last few months I'd worked with him five, sometimes six days a week. He's even moved most of his files upstairs to my office. Now, each morning, whether Jason had arrived or not, I had the pleasure of smelling his cologne. I'd barely stopped myself from asking him which brand he used so I could spray it on my pillow and smell him as I slept.

I'd noticed Jason the day I walked into the Georgia office five years ago. And it mostly had nothing to do with how good looking he was and more to do with his light-up-the-room smile. That's not to say he wasn't downright hot, because he was, but it was his friendliness and laughter that had drawn me to him. Then I noticed his wedding ring and I promptly started to avoid him. Of course he was married, all the good ones normally were. We'd worked a few cases over the years, and I quickly got over my insta-lust crush. A gold band was my number one attraction killer. I didn't look twice at a married man. Not now, not ever. And Jason might as well still have been married. Sure, his wife had passed away, and he'd taken off his ring about a year ago, but there was no doubt the memory of her still kept him warm at night.

The thing about him was, he was no longer open and friendly. Sometimes he could be a downright dick. Yet, somehow that attracted me to him more. Because I knew his piss-poor attitude came from pain. My dad had also called me a "fixer," though I'd long ago gotten over the need to mend the broken people in my life. I'd learned the hard way there was no fixing a person when they were hellbent on self-destruction.

"Mercy?" Jason's rumbly voice pulled me from my thoughts.

"Yeah?"

"You didn't hear a word I said, did you?"

"No. Sorry, I was thinking."

Jason sat down and rolled his chair in front of my desk and leaned back. "Something I can help with? Did the local PD send over the reports you requested?"

Thank God, he thought it was the case that had me so deep in thought. So far, I'd done a damn good job keeping my attraction to him under wraps. The last thing I wanted was him knowing, or worse, feeling uncomfortable around me.

"Yeah, they did. The three students the narc had recommended for a background check came up with nothing. Their parents are clean, too."

The undercover narcotics officer was good. He'd blended in well and made friends quickly.

"Did you read his report?"

"I did. Pretty impressive, he's been out to parties every weekend since he started."

"Yeah, well, it helps he looks like he's sixteen, and I'm sure every girl at that school is drooling over him."

"So, you like 'em young, huh?" Jason chuckled. "Good to know."

My heart skipped a beat, and I think I may have actually stopped breathing. The sound was rusty and a whole lot out of practice but it was definitely a laugh. I didn't think I'd heard the sound in two years.

"Hell no. Especially not ten years younger than me. It doesn't matter how hot the kid is, I'd have to duct tape his mouth after about ten minutes."

"Duct tape, huh? Sounds kinky."

Jason was still smiling and my heart was still pounding.

"I don't know about kinky, but the last thing I want to hear about is the latest boy band that's on tour."

"No NSYNC, then?"

"For the love of all things holy, tell me you didn't listen to NSYNC."

"That would be a hell no." Jason looked down at his watch before he asked, "You ready to go? I thought we could grab a bite to eat before we head to the football game."

"Shit. I forgot about the game. I didn't bring a change of clothes." Tonight, we were supposed to be going to the Polytech football game. The undercover narc, Keith, said there'd been a lot of talk about kids scoring at the games. He requested extra eyes and ears so some of us were going to the game posing as spectators. "I can meet you there."

"Or we can stop by your place and go from there."

"As long as you don't mind." Is what I said. However, inside, I was having a tiny come apart thinking about the huge mess I'd left in my kitchen this morning. I'd been too tired to clean up last night and I'd overslept this morning, meaning there were still last night's takeout wrappers on my counter and dishes in the sink.

"Actually, this works out better. We can take one car to the game."

"Sure."

I stood and gathered my things wondering if it was rude to ask him to wait in his car so he didn't see the disaster that was my house. Not that it should matter. It wasn't like this was a date or something. We were going to a high school football game for a case. It was an assignment for fucks sake, why was I acting like an idiot? Oh, I knew why, because I've had an on again off again crush on Jason for five years. More off than on due to the whole married thing, but, and there was always a but, I couldn't deny the crush was back. Which was stupid because he was one-hundred percent unavailable.

"After you." He motioned for me to precede him out of my office.

He held open the doors for me as we exited, and he walked me to my car, checking the lot as we walked through and even the back seat of my car after I beeped the fob, illuminating the interior. I wanted to laugh. I carried the same shield and gun he did, yet he still waited for me to get into my car, lock the door, and start it before he walked away to get into his vehicle.

I spent the next ten minutes on the drive to my house wishing I lived farther away. There had to be some 1-800 emergency, on call, maid service somewhere that could go to someone's house at a moment's notice to check and make sure you hadn't left a pair of panties on your living room floor. Not that I had panties lying around, at least I hoped I didn't.

All too soon we pulled into my neighborhood, and I prayed Jason wasn't some sort of neat freak. I pulled into my garage and checked my rearview mirror as I turned off the ignition. Sure as shit, he'd gotten out of his car and was walking into my garage.

On an exhale I opened my door.

Here goes nothing.

3

WHAT THE HELL was I doing? I should've waited in my car while she changed to go to the game. Actually, I should've just met her there. But, for some stupid reason, I'd suggested we not only go get something to eat before the game but we take one car.

"I'll just be a second." Her voice sounded a bit nervous and why shouldn't it? I was basically a stranger and I'd just invited myself into her home. I was getting ready to tell her I was going to wait outside when she stopped at the door and turned to face me. "Listen. Before we go in, I've been totally caught up in this case and everything else has fallen to the wayside."

"Okay." I wasn't exactly sure what she was trying to tell me, but it seemed to mean something to her.

I obviously hadn't given her the response she wanted if her sigh and eyeroll were any indication.

"My house is a freaking disaster. I don't want you to think I'm a slob. I mean, I am, but not a dirty one."

"Is there a difference?"

"Yes!" she huffed. "A big difference. There's shit everywhere, but it's clean shit. Like clutter. Not gross shit, like mold. Okay, there may be some trash on the counters, too. But I'm not growing science experiments or anything."

There was an unusual tic in my cheek and something that felt a lot like a smile pulled on my lips.

"Now, I gotta see what 'clean shit' looks like."

"I'm serious, Jason."

"I am, too, Mercy. Open the door."

I wasn't sure why she cared what I thought about the state of her home, but, clearly, she did.

"I haven't cleaned out my fridge in over a month. I think there's pizza in there from two weeks ago. I would never judge you because your house is dirty." Her perfectly shaped left brow lifted, calling me on my lie. "Okay. I would totally judge you if there were thirty-two cats living in there and you had litter boxes all over the house. I also might not sit down. Or eat anything."

"I don't have a cat." She smiled her light-up-the-room smile. I'd been noticing way too much about her lately. The way she wore heels on Mondays and Fridays but not the other days of the week. She preferred Diet Coke over regular and drank more coffee than anyone I'd ever known. She also lived off of sugar, which was damn impressive considering she had a body . . . what the fuck?

I shook my head to dislodge the improper thoughts and waited for her to open the door.

"I swear I'll be quick," she told me once we'd entered and she tossed her cell phone and keys on the counter.

"No alarm?" I asked when she unclipped her shield and pulled her duty holster free from the waistband of her slacks.

"No." She placed her gun on the counter and put her hand on her hip. "Before I leave the room, do I need to talk to you about gun safety and tell you never to touch a loaded weapon?" she teased.

"Is that a speech you have to give often?" I was joking but why was there a twinge of jealousy tied up in those words?

"Funny."

"Funny, ha-ha? Or funny because it's true?" Why the fuck was I pressing for an answer? "I'm kidding. Hurry and get changed, I'm starving." I tried to cover up my out of character behavior.

She hurried out of the room, leaving me alone in her kitchen. It was nowhere near as bad as she'd made it sound. There were a few dishes in the sink and some drive-thru bags on the counter, but it wasn't the pigsty she'd made it out to be. I wondered if someone from her past had harped on her about clutter. There were also some stacks of papers here and there, but she was right, it was clean shit lying around. Women confused me, they worried too much about stupid stuff that no one cared about. I peeked into the living room and there were shoes on the floor and some books stacked on the coffee table along with remotes. Her house was lived in. It was warm and inviting. I could imagine her coming home from a long day and plopping down on her couch, putting her feet up and watching TV.

The unmistakable, over-autotuned voice of Britney Spears blared from Mercy's phone and I wasn't sure if I was in a state of shock or panic.

"Shit!" Mercy yelled from her bedroom. "Please hit the ignore button on my phone."

Thank God. If I had to hear "oh, baby, baby" one more time I may have had to shoot her phone. I swiped the ignore button, ending the call and not even two seconds later it rang again.

"For fucks sakes. She'll just keep calling. Please answer it and tell her I'll call her later."

It was an odd request, however, if it meant it would end my suffering, I'd do it.

I slid the green call button and before I even had the phone to my ear, I heard a woman speaking. "I have an emergency and you send me to voicemail? That's low. Quick, second date tonight, my blue strapless with the silver heels or my LBD with the gold strappy sandals? I don't want to scream easy but I don't wanna look like a nun either."

What the hell was happening?

"Hello. Earth to Mercy! Blue or black?"

"This isn't Mercy." Before I could get anything else out the woman all but screeched.

"Who the hell are you and why are you answering Mercy's phone? And don't lie to me, I can track her phone. I have an app for that."

"Well, since you have an app and all, she's changing."

"Changing? Who is this?"

"Jason Walker. I work with Mercy."

"I know who you are."

I wanted to ask how she knew who I was but I didn't. The conversation was weird enough. "Good, then you know she's safe and sound."

Mercy came rushing into the room, hopping on one foot trying to shove her other foot into a sneaker. She'd pulled her long hair up into a ponytail and her face was as red as a beet.

"Here's Mercy." I started to hand the phone over before I pulled it back. "For the record, go with whichever dress covers more."

"Covers more? Did you miss the part where I said I didn't want to look like a nun?"

"Men like to be teased. To have to use their imagination. So cover up," I told her.

"Right. And the shoes?"

"The sexier of the two."

"Awesome. Thanks. Tell Mer I'll call her tomorrow. I have five minutes to get dressed. Bye, Jason Walker."

She hung up. Weirdest fucking conversation I'd ever had in my life.

"Who was that?" I asked, as I set Mercy's phone back on the counter.

"That was Tuesday."

"Tuesday?"

"That's her name. She's a five-foot-nine ball of crazy. When we were in high school, she was an honest-to-God runway model. Sorry again about asking you to answer that. She has no boundaries and will call over and over until I answer." Her words may've sounded like Tuesday annoyed her, but she was smiling huge. "She's my best friend. Well, my only real friend, actually."

"You're not going to ask what she wanted?"

"Don't need to. It's Friday night, second date with Len, and I heard you telling her what to wear. I assume two back-to-back calls were because she was in full-on meltdown mode not knowing what to wear."

"You'd be right. She do that often?"

"Do what? The second date thing or the meltdowns?"

"Right. She does both frequently."

"Right you are. Ready to go?"

This was starting out to be a bizarre evening all the way around, but strangely it was the most fun I'd had in years. Wasn't that some shit? I was a thirty-year-old man and I considered going to a co-worker's home and talking to her best friend fun. *Christ, when had my life turned to this?* The niggling guilt slammed into my chest, reminding me I had no business going anywhere or doing anything fun. We were working on a case, not playing grab ass.

"Yeah. Let's go."

4

SOMETHING WAS OFF.

Jason had gone from smiling to stoic in two-point-five seconds. He wasn't being mean, or a jerk, or necessarily quiet. He'd talked on the way to the burger place next to the high school. He was polite, made small talk while we waited for our food, but the conversation was work related. He hadn't even commented on Tuesday's ringtone. Come on, what sane person wouldn't make fun of me for having a Britney Spears ringtone? Especially after I'd asked him if he listened to boy bands.

When our check came, he pulled out cash and refused to allow me to pay my half. We should've taken the bill and expensed it, but he blew that off, too. The shift was strange and it was starting to give me a complex. Was it me? Was my house not tidy enough? Did Tuesday piss him off?

"Listen, I'm really sorry about Tuesday. I hope she didn't annoy you or something."

"She didn't."

"So, is something else bothering you?"

"No. Why?"

"I don't know. You seem a little frosty since we left my house."

The pain that flashed in his eyes took my breath, and I wished I could pull my careless words back. The emotion was quickly masked, and I was fast learning he'd perfected the look. You know the one? The look of indifference. Once upon a time, I, too, had been so caught up in my grief I'd taught myself to be emotionless. Blank. Giving nothing to no one was easier.

"Didn't realize talking about an ongoing investigation was considered frosty."

"Never mind. Sorry."

"We should get to the game."

Well, that ended that conversation, and now me and my big mouth had made things uncomfortable. He was practically a mute on the way to the high school. The few times I'd asked his thoughts on the case or ran a scenario by him he used the least amount of words possible to answer. My lack of filter kicked in one more time as we were walking to the stadium.

"I shouldn't have said anything—"

"It's fine."

"I mean—"

Jason stopped and turned toward me. He was a good six inches taller than me, but with a scowl on his face and looking down at me, I would've sworn on a stack of bibles he was six-feet taller. He looked like one pissed off man.

"Drop it."

"Okay."

He turned and walked off in the direction of the bleachers. My stomach dropped, and I wished at some point in my life I'd learned to keep my trap shut.

"You coming?"

I didn't answer, I just moved. No more talking for me, God knows, I'd done enough for one night. He found us seats next to a group of kids and helped me sit. It would've been a lot easier to ignore my silly infatuation if he'd stop doing little things that made me like him more.

The game started, and we both were concentrating on the conversations around us. Trying to eavesdrop while fans cheered all around was not the easiest task. But I'd heard the kids behind us mentioning a girl named Stella would be at a party and she had the *hook up*. I'd also heard one of the girls saying she was going to try to get Keith alone tonight and, by the way Jason stiffened next to me, he'd heard it, too. The more the teenager went on about how she was going to corner the undercover narc, the more I was worried for him. And not because I was afraid Keith would cross the line with an underage girl, it was all the ways she had planned to get what she wanted from him.

"Shit," Jason mumbled.

Shit was right. Her fail-proof plan included spiking his drink with ecstasy.

I yanked my phone out of my bag and sent Keith a text warning him of the teenager's plan and about Stella being there.

His emoji text back had me shaking my head. The stupid okay sign a clear indication my original assessment of the age gap was correct.

Jason glanced at my phone and lifted his chin in question. I turned the screen so he could see and he actually smiled.

"I guess your plan to use duct tape wouldn't work so well in today's text-only world. I'd say you'd need to tape his fingers together, but you might want him to use those."

I couldn't believe he'd said that. Not that it wasn't funny, because it was. But I'd never heard Jason make an inappropriate joke. I had my quip locked and loaded but I opted to keep my mouth shut. I'd already put my foot in it too many times tonight. And it was a crap shoot whether or not he'd get my sense of humor. Most people didn't, staying quiet was my best option.

After a few moments he knocked his shoulder into mine and said, "Nothing? Really?"

"Oh, I have plenty. I'm just a little surprised I'd have to explain to you that if tape was needed on his hands to prevent him from emojiing me to death that would leave his mouth free, therefore I wouldn't need his fingers."

His head tipped, and he barked out a laugh. I was so enthralled with the way the muscles in his neck bunched I'd missed the sound entirely. I wasn't sure what he'd found funny, the fact I'd said "emojiing" which I was pretty sure wasn't in the Oxford dictionary or that I was alluding to being eaten out. The more I thought about what I'd said, the more I couldn't believe I'd said it. Well, I could, I said stupid shit all the time. I just couldn't believe I'd said it to him.

"At this point, I don't think I'd know what to do with either."

Holy dear God in heaven above, he just said that?

"Eh. I'm sure it's like riding a bike. Once you hop on the seat and start pumping away it will all come back to you."

My hand flew to my mouth like I had to physically restrain it from embarrassing me further. Who needed their mouth duct taped shut now? Sheesh, I was such a fucking idiot.

This time when he laughed, I closed my eyes and

listened. The sound was magical. A mythical noise that he'd kept hidden for so long. Damn, he had a great laugh, but I was never speaking again. I needed to have my mouth wired shut when I was near him.

"Damn, you're funny."

Unfortunately, the look on his face wasn't. Hot. Cold. Smiling. Sad. His emotions were making me sea sick.

5

"WALKER. James. We need you in the conference room," Bruce Adams called into Mercy's office on his way past.

"You know what that's about?" she asked.

"Nope."

Bruce was our narc's handler. He was also a damn good detective. He was the head of the drug task force for the county. He was one of the few cops that welcomed the help of the DEA. There was a reason we had an office in this area. The I-95 corridor was one of the most heavily used freight routes in the US. It spans from Canada to the tip of Florida. With the ease of the major interstate it also meant drugs were also easily trafficked. When the DEA moved into the area, we were met by some resistance. But Bruce Adams saw a chance to get drugs off the streets. He didn't care who got the credit, or which agency's numbers got a bump in bringing in a large bust. His only interest was to stop drug deals and to prevent more deaths. I respected the hell out of him.

Mercy quickly grabbed her notebook and files and disappeared from her office. Why the hell was I still working upstairs in her office? I had a perfectly good one downstairs. I had an actual desk in there, too, not a cramped side table. When I first started working in Mercy's office it was out of convenience. We were talking the case out, sharing information, going over reports, and planning the operation. Now I'd settled into a routine of coming up here, working next to her, and talking to her throughout the day. Either I'd pick up lunch and bring it back or she would. We'd eat in her office together, talking and laughing about non-case related stuff. And, sometimes, we'd even gone out to eat together. It was easy to be around her. Too easy, as a matter of fact. I liked her, she made me feel normal, like my old self. Our conversations were always light, we'd never discussed our private lives. She'd never asked about my family, and I never inquired about hers. The only thing that came close to being personal was Tuesday. We'd talked about her second date, what she'd worn, what happened, and how she'd already gone on a first date with someone new in the two weeks since the football game.

I wanted to ask why Mercy never went out on any dates, but thought better of it. Maybe she *was* dating, hell maybe she had a serious, steady boyfriend. She was a beautiful woman, and I imagined there were men lining up for the chance to take her out. She was quirky and funny, too. She was also brash and had no filter. She blurted out whatever was on her mind, consequences and hurt feelings be damned. I actually liked that best about her. You always knew where you stood with Mercy James, she didn't pull punches. When she thought someone was wrong, she said so, then she backed up her reasoning with facts. She was a breath of fresh air in my polluted world.

After today, I had to get away from her and go back to working in my office. If I needed something I could come up here. I'd been telling myself it was out of laziness, not wanting to walk up a flight of stairs, that I was staying in her office. The lie was easier to swallow than the truth. Because acknowledging the truth meant admitting I enjoyed her company.

"You coming?" Scott Mann, another SA working the case, asked.

"Yeah. Right behind you."

I stood and looked around Mercy's office. Much like her home it was organized clutter. Clean shit, as she called it. Her life, her living space were so much different than my own. You could feel her personality all around you. Not in mine. Mine was devoid of any signs of life.

By the time I'd made it to the conference room Mercy and Bruce were in deep discussion. They were sitting close together looking over surveillance photos. Scott, Ellen Mckenna, and Paul Hollman, all agents from the building, were sitting, waiting to start. I took the seat farthest from Mercy and Bruce and tried my best not to stare at the duo. I had no right to feel the jealousy that was bubbling up. I had no claim on her time or attention. Yet, it still pissed me off.

Bruce stood and walked to a large, rolling white board and pointed to a picture of a teenage girl.

"Stella Jones. Keith was able to track her down and confirm she was there selling her Adderall. Her parents have been notified, and they confirmed her prescription had been filled that day, so she had a thirty-day supply to unload. Not surprising, she'd sold the entire bottle at the party."

Bruce moved to the next picture and pointed to it. "Meet Emma Lucas. Seventeen, a senior, average student, middle-class family, and girls field hockey player. She ewas the one planning on seducing Officer Michaels. Damn good catch, James and Walker. I don't think Officer Michaels would've drunk anything at the party, but shit happens, and you prevented a possible clusterfuck. He poured the drink into a flask and was able to get it to the lab. Toxicology came back, gamma butyrolactone, or GBL. There was also a high dosage of sildenafil."

"Jesus, was she trying to kill him?" Scott asked.

"She was trying to do something, my guess, trying to get laid," Paul added.

Spiking a drink with a date rape drug and adding an erectile dysfunction medication could have deadly results.

"What are we doing with Emma?" I inquired.

"Emma is Keith's new girlfriend. He's keeping her close."

"And how is that going to work? The girl obviously wants sex. She's not going to take no for an answer. We're putting Keith in a no-win situation."

Mercy said exactly what I was thinking. Going undercover was always hard, but working in a high school around minors was much more difficult. You walked a tight rope of impropriety every day. He had to blend in, talk like them, act like them, but he still had to follow the law—to the letter. If this girl was after him sexually, that was a problem, a big one. And as much as Emma was caught up in a drug investigation she was still a child and needed to be handled with care.

"He has it covered. We've fitted him, his car, and his locker with cameras. Every time he's with her, we'll have eyes and ears. He's protected, believe me he's not thrilled to have to even hold the girl's hand, but he's committed. He thinks there's more at play than a bunch of high schoolers wanting to get high and have sex. Someone is supplying them with the drugs."

I did not envy Keith or the position we were putting him in. The faster we worked this case the sooner he'd be out of it. And the sooner I could get away from Mercy and get back to my cases.

6

"NESSA KULAR. Reported missing yesterday after she didn't come home from a sleepover Saturday night. She was supposed to be with a group of friends at Mary Beth Stevens's house. The Stevenses said there was no sleepover at their house," I rattled off what Detective Adams had sent me.

Let's just say, my new number one worst way to start a Monday was a six a.m. callout. Okay, the callout wasn't what I hated, looking down at a pretty, fourteen-year-old dead girl was. COD suspected drug overdose. A morning jogger had found her at a park. The only reason the passerby discovered her was because her dog had gone into the bushes and wouldn't come out.

"Parkside High School. Freshman—"

"Wait. Did you say Parkside?" Jason asked.

"Yeah."

"Fuck. My sister, Delaney's a teacher there."

"You have a sister?"

Weird question to ask while standing over a dead body, but I'd been taken aback. First, because I hadn't known he had a sister, and, second, because he'd shared something personal, which he never did. There were these invisible walls around our friendship. Inside of those walls were things we could freely talk about. Like movies, food, the news, the weather. You know, inconsequential shit that you'd talk to your deli counter clerk about. Then there was everything else. That stuff was outside the perimeter and no-go topics. Family, life, goals, dreams, the past, the wife.

"I have four. Delaney is the oldest. Then there's Quinn, and the youngest are the twins, Hadley and Adalynn."

Perhaps his morning coffee hadn't kicked in yet or he'd forgotten to electrify the fence he lived behind, because that one sentence gave me more information about him than all of the other sentences combined over the last four months we'd been working this case together. Not that I'd told him anything about myself, but that was only because I knew in doing so, I'd make him shut down.

Jason was no longer looking around the area, he was on his phone. Truthfully, there was nothing for us to do here. Adams had only called us to the scene to keep us in the loop. He believed in sharing every piece of the puzzle. Even the small stuff the DEA had no jurisdiction over.

"Delaney said she has first period free. If we hurry we can go and talk to her before her classes start."

"Did you tell her why you wanted to see her?"

"No, she thinks it's a brotherly visit."

The sadness was back, and I wondered if he and his sisters were close, or if he had other family in the area. Not that I was going to ask.

We said our goodbyes to the detectives on the scene and made our way to the street.

"I'm right here, want to drive over with me?" he asked, but it really wasn't a question considering he'd already opened the passenger side door for me.

Once we were on the road he asked, "Do you have any siblings?"

"No."

I didn't elaborate or offer any more information. Just because he felt chatty at the moment didn't mean he wouldn't change his mind, and talking about my brother Neil and how I'd lost him wasn't something I was willing to share. Not while Jason was still giving me whiplash.

"Do all your sisters live around here?"

"Yes. Hadley and Adalynn are both in college, they're twenty. Quinn is and always has been the wild child. She's twenty-three and still trying to find herself."

"Nothing wrong with that. She's figuring herself out, and that's actually a good thing."

"I suppose. She drives my dad crazy. One minute she wants to be a flight attendant to see the world, the next she's going to school to be an ultrasound tech. Then there was the time she was going to join the Peace Corps. I think that's the only thing he ever flat-out forbade her to do."

"Why?"

"Because he was in the military and he had first-hand experience with what goes on in third world countries. And while the Peace Corps is a great program, it's not right for my sister. She has no sense of situational awareness and is often too trusting. It was a recipe for disaster."

"Sounds familiar."

I hadn't meant to say that out loud. I didn't know Quinn and Jason's dad was probably correct, the Peace Corps may have been dangerous for someone like Quinn, but I still bristled at the notion.

"What does that mean?"

"Nothing. Do you think there's a connection to Nessa and the Polytech parties?"

"Tell me what you meant," he demanded.

So much for the ban on exchanging personal information. There was no way for me to answer his question without explaining my father and my family situation.

"It just means, I heard something similar when I was growing up. And when I decided to join the DEA it was met with resistance."

"I don't understand. Your instincts are spot on; you're a great agent."

His praise felt good. I'd worked my ass off, not to prove I could be just as good as the men I worked with, or to prove to my father I could do it. I worked hard for myself. I took pride in my work ethic and abilities. I'd learned a long time ago the only person's opinion that matter was mine. Day in and day out I competed with myself. Only I knew if I was giving my job a hundred percent. Only I knew if I was living my life the way I wanted to. And I was the only one responsible for my happiness.

"Thanks."

"So, tell me, who told you you couldn't do the job?"

"Why, Jason? We don't talk about this kind of stuff. We keep our private lives separate from our professional relationship. The who and the reasons why lean toward personal."

"Is there a reason you don't want to share personal information?"

Was he crazy? The separation was his doing. I was

mostly an open book. I owned my past. Owned my mistakes. And owned my grief. He hid behind his, pretending like the past didn't exist.

"Me? No. But anything beyond an easy discussion seems to bother you. I'm just curious why you want to know now."

"I just do." His answer was tight and to the point.

"My dad was a cop. He was extremely strict. After so many years on the job he was jaded. There were bad guys around every corner. I guess in some ways he was right. Anyway, I was probably a little like Quinn. I was a daredevil and had no fear. I was pretty much the same person at ten that I am now. I never understood why people sugarcoated the truth, I blurted out whatever was on my mind. As I got older and learned how short life was, I decided nothing was going to stop me from living. My dad always told me I had no sense of self-preservation and I was too impulsive. I do what I want, when I want, and I'll rise to any challenge put in front of me. He hated it. He didn't want me to go into any type of law enforcement. He said I was signing my own death certificate."

"And what did your mom say?"

"My mom's dead. She died having me. And while my dad did his best, I always wondered if he blamed me for her dying. He never said it, and I knew he loved me, but he always told me stories about how he met my mom and how it was love at first sight. He never remarried, or dated, he lived a very lonely life."

I probably shouldn't have added the last part, considering Jason's situation, but it was the truth and I wasn't known for my tact. My dad died alone. He never got over my mom's death, never accepted love from another person. He said he was happy and his only desire was to raise me and Neil. But he couldn't hide from me and my brother. We both knew he was lonely.

"Jesus, Mercy, that's horrible."

I did notice he didn't say he was sorry.

"It pretty much sucked not growing up with a mom." He'd pulled in front of the school and parked.

"Hopefully, your sister will be able to tell us something about Nessa."

"Yeah, maybe."

And the frosty Jason was back. Or maybe this was the appalled Jason. Growing up I had two choices, sulk and be sad over not having a mom or make the best out of what I had. I chose then and still choose now to make the best out of life. It can all be over in the blink of an eye.

7

I WAS REELING from what Mercy had told me. I couldn't imagine growing up without a mom. My parents had played such an important role in my life, I couldn't begin to picture a world without them. I was also a whole lot taken aback by the way she'd told me. I guess I shouldn't have been, she'd told me about her mother's death like she did everything else, to the point, factual, and nothing more. I was beginning to wonder if Mercy had any feelings. I had yet to see any real emotion come from her.

And now she was looking at me like I was the one who'd dropped a bomb. I suppose she was correct when she'd said I didn't ask personal questions. I didn't, because I didn't want to have to answer any. The only reason I'd brought up Delaney was because Nessa was a student at the school my sister taught at.

There was a chance she could give us some information and there was the added benefit I got to warn her to keep her eyes open and stay safe. What I didn't need to do was ask her if she had any siblings or push her to tell me about her family. I don't know why I did it, maybe it was because I was too comfortable around her. The easy comradery made me forget.

It had been days since I'd decided I needed to go back to my own office yet I was still in hers. We stopped at the front entrance of the school, and I pressed the intercom and waited until the school's secretary asked for our names. The locks clicked open after she told us to check in with the office.

"Well, at least they keep the doors locked now," Mercy muttered. "Something is better than nothing."

There was nothing to say to that. She was right, it was better than an open campus, but with all the recent school shootings I was still worried about Delaney.

We signed in at the front office and made our way to my sister's classroom. She stood up from behind her desk and smiled.

"Jason."

Yes, she was my sister, but I couldn't miss she was a beautiful woman. My dad had always said he was being punished for every bad deed in his past when all four of his daughters turned out looking like my mom.

He wasn't wrong. They all had jet-black hair like her, only their eye colors varied. Delaney and I got my mom's blue eyes. Quinn and the twins got my dad's eyes, which, on my sisters, meant they had striking green eyes that were no less pretty than Delaney's blue ones. I'd heard how hot my mom was my whole life, which was disgusting for any son to hear. The comments had led to more than one fight. And when my sisters got older, I'd threatened dozens of teenage boys to stay the fuck away from them. It didn't matter I was ten years older than the twins and I was intimidating minors.

"Hey, sis. This is Special Agent Mercy James."

"Hi, Mercy, nice to meet you." She offered her hand to Mercy. "So this isn't a social visit then?"

I hated how my sister's smile fell. One more thing to feel like shit about. I'd pulled away from my close-knit family. Mainly because we were close-knit. That meant they pried. It was a shitty thing to think, but they asked questions and wanted to talk about stuff I wanted to bury.

"Nice to meet you, Delaney. Unfortunately, no. We need some help on a case and were hoping we could ask you a few questions."

"Sure. I'd offer you a seat, but all I have to offer are desks."

"We'll stand. Do you know a student named Nessa

Kular?"

Mercy had taken over the conversation, and I was grateful. It'd been weeks or maybe even over a month since I'd seen my sister, and my heart hurt. There was a time we'd all gathered once a week for family dinners. Then there were the get togethers almost monthly at one of my uncles' houses. It was widely known you didn't miss a family function. I'd been given a wide berth after Kayla died, everyone had wanted to give me time to grieve. But as the months slid by, I began to take advantage of the pass. When my dad and uncles had come around and told me to snap out of it, I'd blown them off. It was so fucked up. I was fucked up. Now the chasm was so wide I wasn't sure how to fix it.

"I do. She's in my third period algebra class. There are only two of us that teach freshman math. She's a pretty good student. Doesn't turn in her homework, which isn't unusual but she still scores well on quizzes and tests. She's very popular. Most teenage girls are more focused on their social standing than on school-work, but she's almost desperate for it."

"What do you mean?" I cut in.

"I'm around teenagers all day long. I watch how they interact with each other. It's hard to put into words, more of a gut feeling."

"Your gut is very rarely wrong, Delaney. What gave you the impression she was desperate?"

"You know how when you were a kid and you were told you couldn't do something or go somewhere, you'd be ticked off? But it was a minor irritation not an over-the-top end of the world explosion."

"Like, if Mom and Dad said you couldn't go to the movies, you'd argue with them because you wanted to go but you wouldn't have had an all-out tantrum or be extremely anxious you couldn't go?" I supplied.

"Right. Well, there were a few times I wanted Nessa to come in during lunch to do her missing homework. She didn't simply argue like the rest of the kids. She was agitated and on the verge of a panic attack."

"Did she tell you why?"

"She gave me a bullshit reason about being hungry and wanting to eat. Which, just so you know, the kids who need to come to my class during lunch bring their food. I did overhear her telling one of her friends, Cherie Anderson, not to let anyone sit next to Jeff. It wasn't that she didn't want anyone sitting next to the boy that caught my attention, it was that she sounded desperate."

"Do you know who this Jeff boy is?"

"No. I don't have any Jeffs in any of my classes. Is she in trouble?"

"She was found dead this morning," I told her.

"Damn. Has anyone notified the school?"

"No. Word's going to get out before the PD gets

here to talk to the principal. It always does. But do me a favor? Keep your eyes open. Any kids acting strangely, let me know."

"As soon as this gets around, everyone will be acting strangely. I hate to say it, but everyone will suddenly be her best friend. Even the kids that were mean to her or didn't like her will act like they were BFFs."

"You're right about that," Mercy said. "Listen for any talk of parties she went to this weekend. Or any parties Mary Beth Stevens attended."

My sister shook her head, and her eyes widened. "The Stevens girl is bad news. I wouldn't be surprised if the party was actually at her house."

"Her parents said the sleepover the other girls told their parents about didn't happen in their home."

"Right. Says the rich parents who leave their four-teen-year-old home for the weekend alone so they can go out of town. I'd check their credit cards to make sure they were home this weekend."

"How do you know that?"

"Teenagers are stupid. They don't pay attention to who's around them when they make their weekend party plans. I hear all about it. Most nights when I leave here, I wish ear bleach was a real thing, because girls nowadays are doing things I didn't do until college."

"I don't want to know." I held up my hand, stopping my sister from elaborating further. I knew for a fact she'd only been with one guy. And he was one of my closest friends. I didn't want the details of her and Carter Lenox's sex life or I'd rethink kicking his Navy SEAL ass.

"You don't. Trust me. Sometimes I feel like we're back in the 60s with free love, drugs, and rock 'n' roll. These kids are far too sexually active and open to using an assortment of whatever drugs they can get their hands on.

"How did Nessa die?"

"Suspected OD," Mercy answered.

"I hate to say it, but that's not surprising."

"Why haven't you ever told me what's going on in your school? I work for the fucking DEA."

"I don't know, Jason, why haven't I?" Delaney's glare was lethal. "You've been a tad . . . preoccupied the last few years. And not to mention, my school isn't any worse than any other. It's not like bricks of coke are flowing through the halls."

Welp, I'd opened the door and stepped in shit. I deserved that and more. But I didn't want to have this argument in front of Mercy.

"Thanks for the information; we'll let you get back to work."

"Sure."

She and Mercy exchanged pleasantries, and, just when I thought I was out of the woods, my sister went for the kill shot.

"Oh, and, Jason, maybe you can stop by Mom and Dad's next week for dinner. Hadley and Adalynn's twenty-first is coming up and the 'rents are planning a blow out, your input would be welcomed."

"Thanks, I'll try."

"I'd try real hard, brother. Word is you're on a short rope."

My ire got the best of me when I turned to scowl at my sister. Much to my dismay, the look no longer worked like it did when I wanted her out of my room when we were kids. "How about we not do this now, and you let me worry about my personal life."

"There's never a good time for you. Never will be either. Wake up, you're being a selfish prick, and your bullshit is affecting the whole family. Namely Mom. And we all know what happens when Mom's upset."

"My bullshit?"

My sister had some nerve calling my wife dying bullshit.

Delaney's eyes slid to Mercy before they came back to me. They were softer now, but it was too late, she'd overstepped. "It's time. It's been over two years. We all miss—"

"Don't you say it."

"But we miss you, too. Enough hiding."

"I'm not hiding from anything. I have work to do, and you have classes to teach. I'll talk to you later."

Damn, I didn't need another lecture and I really didn't want to know what a short rope meant. Maybe I should just start going to Sunday dinners again. I could sit and smile and pretend life was terrific for two hours a week. At least it would make my mom feel better. And if my mom was happy everyone else would be, too.

After storming out of the school, I waited by the car for a long time before Mercy finally came out. Great, she was pissed, as well. I didn't understand what the hell she had the right to be mad about. It wasn't her sister who'd just embarrassed the living hell out of her. And Delaney had almost said it, the name was on the tip of her tongue. I didn't want to hear Kayla's name when I was awake. God knows, I heard enough in my sleep. Every goddamn night I live our life together over again in my dreams. It was a never-ending movie reminding me of all the ways I'd failed my wife. All the ways I'd failed our love.

No, I didn't want to talk about Kayla or how she was planning on leaving me. How my wife had fallen out of love with me. I was a fucking shit husband and a failure.

8

TO SAY Jason was pissed would be the understatement of the year. After he'd stomped out of his sister's classroom she'd apologized profusely for her behavior. I didn't see anything wrong with what she'd said to Jason. As a matter of fact, it sounded like it was long overdue. He was silent on the drive back to the office. He went straight to his office and slammed the door. I went up to mine, not interested in his antics.

I sounded like a stone-cold bitch but I understood more than he realized. I knew what it was like to lose someone you love in the most horrific way. But what I couldn't understand was why he'd shut out his family. The people who loved him and wanted to support him. What I wouldn't have given to have had family around me when I'd needed them. Instead, I'd been all alone in my sadness and anger. Again, two choices—lie down and take it or rise above. I was all I had, there was no lying down for me.

I plopped down in my chair and tried to forget about the excruciating look of pain on Jason's face. I dove into work, hoping it would distract me from wanting to go and check on Jason. The desire was a direct contradiction to my earlier annoyance, but the thought of him suffering alone in his office bothered me, even if it was his own doing. I needed to get my head in the game, there was another dead teen, and if we didn't want more on our hands, we needed to shut this down. I was going over all the toxicology reports when Detective Adams poked his head in.

"Got a minute?"

"Sure."

"The tox screen came back on Nessa Kular. High levels of GHB. All consistent with the other reports, the chemical composition is the same. And the same compounds as the GBL found in the concoction Emma made for Keith, 1, 4-butanediol."

"Jesus Christ, these kids are making GHL from industrial cleaner?"

Gamma butyrolactone turned into GHB when ingested. Which was why the liquid Keith gave the lab was GHL but the tox reports on the dead teenagers came up with gamma hydroxybutyrate in their systems. Bottom line was someone had found a recipe to make a potentially deadly sex drug.

"Yes. My guys are tracking down any shipments of cleaners containing 1, 4-butyrolactone. Good news is there are secondary chemicals present. The lab narrowed it down to ink solvent. Bad news is you can buy it at any Walmart or office supply warehouse."

"So what you're telling me is, tracking down a shipment is going to be a dead end?"

"Pretty much, yes. We need to find out who's making it."

"With the internet anyone with the desire can find any recipe to manufacture any drug."

The knock on the doorframe nearly had me jumping out of my seat. I'd been so engrossed in reading over the report Bruce had handed me I hadn't heard anyone approach.

"Didn't mean to interrupt, but Delaney texted me. Mary Beth wasn't in school today. Word is she's in the hospital," Jason said.

"The Stevens girl?" Bruce asked.

"Yes. We went to speak to one of Nessa's teachers this morning. She said Mary Beth's house is a known party house. Her parents frequently leave her unattended."

"Thanks for the heads-up. I'll run their credit cards to see where they were this weekend."

"Are you gonna have someone check on Mary Beth's whereabouts, or should we start calling local hospitals?"

"I'll make a few calls. You wanna go with me to interview the Stevenses again? Maybe we can grab some lunch after?" Bruce smiled and I didn't have to look over at Jason to know he was glowering. Annoyance was pouring out of him in waves. Not that he had anything to be frustrated about.

"Wish I could, but I'm behind on filing these reports. You know how Monday mornings are."

"Unfortunately, I do. Some other time then?"

"Sounds good. Call me if you track down Mary Beth."

"Will do."

Bruce turned to leave, shaking Jason's hand before he left my office.

"What's up, Jason?"

I still hadn't looked up at him, for some stupid reason I was nervous at what I'd find. I heard the door click shut and the snap of the blinds being pulled shut, and my heartrate spiked.

"Does Bruce often hand deliver tox reports?"

That was not what I was expecting and the accusatory tone pissed me off. "Sometimes."

"And you don't find that odd?"

Now I was mad. I stood up and walked around my desk. Leaning on the edge, I asked my own question. "Why are you asking?"

"Just trying to figure out if this is the first time he's asked you out."

What in the ever-loving hell was he talking about? I'd been working with Bruce for years. Never had he expressed any interest in me. He was friendly but had never made a pass at me.

"You've lost your mind. He was not asking me out on a date, and, if he was, I'm not sure what business it would be of yours."

"That was him asking you out, Mercy."

"Fine. Say he was asking me out. Again, I'm unclear why that would bother you or what business it is of yours."

"It bothers me."

Whoa. What? It bothered him? I was still trying to gather my thoughts and formulate a retort to his declaration when he stalked toward me. His blue eyes narrowed and his lips pinched together in two flat lines.

"It's none of your—"

My statement was cut off when his hands went to my face, holding me in place, and his mouth slammed onto mine. I was in such a state of shock I stood frozen until his tongue licked the seam of my lips, and I automatically opened for him. There was nothing soft about his kiss, it was punishing and brutal. But it was so damn good my legs wobbled. He took and took, devouring me, and I happily let him. When he pulled away, our eyes locked, and I wished I knew what he was thinking, but he was so good at hiding his emotions I didn't have the first clue. His grip on my face loosened, and he leaned in, this time placing a feather light peck on my lips before he walked out of my office.

I must've stood cemented in place for a good five minutes before I finally went back to work. What in the actual fuck was that? He'd kissed me. Jason Walker had marched his happy ass across the room and planted a spectacular kiss on me. Then he'd left. Just walked out the door without so much as a have a nice day. And I'd let him, and, what was worse, I'd let him do it again.

The rest of the day had passed by in a blur. Bruce had gotten in contact with the Stevens family and Mary Beth was indeed at the hospital. Her father said she had the flu and he'd taken her in as a precaution. Without a warrant we couldn't demand a blood test and we didn't have enough to petition a judge, so Bruce decided not to bother. What he was able to do was interview the mom while she was home alone. The mom was sticking to the story: they were home all weekend, and Mary Beth had never left the house. While his partner continued to speak to the woman, he'd excused himself to use the restroom. With very limited time he'd searched where he could but hadn't found any cleaners containing the chemicals he was looking for.

After I finished the paperwork I was behind on and finished going over Keith's reports I watched the videos from the narc's body cam. The more I watched the more thankful I was to be out of high school and not have any teenaged children. I knew I was bad in high school, and so were my friends, but we weren't this bad. Not even close. The girl, Emma, had deployed a full-court press to get into Keith's boxer shorts. I had to hand it to him, he was handling it like a champ. He'd given her one reason after another as to why he wanted to wait. The problem was, each excuse made him more likable. Like when he told her she was too special to have sex with at a noisy party. Or when he told her he wanted her to know he liked her for more than her pretty smile. Those excuses made a seventeen-year-old's inexperienced heart swoon. Now the girl thought she was in love, where before she just wanted to be the first girl at Polytech to have sex with him. She'd said that. It was in his report. She and her friends were the welcoming committee. She'd even offered to invite one of her friends to join them. I wanted to gag, and Keith's handwritten notes were all in capitals where he'd scribbled she needed professional help for her low self-esteem.

By the time I was done for the day, I was DONE. All I wanted to do was go home, curl up on the couch, and not think about drugs and teen sex. When I passed Jason's office, it was empty and the lights were off. My stomach clenched. It had been months since Jason had left without saying goodnight or walking me to my car. It was odd how I'd gotten used to the routine. It wouldn't be long before the case was wrapped up and he'd go back to the trafficking task force and we'd barely cross paths again. I shouldn't have let myself get so wrapped up in him in the first place. I'd been so deep in thought on the way home I forgot to drive through Micky D's and pick up dinner.

Screw going back out, there had to be something unhealthy in my house to eat. Too tired to look, I tossed my shit on the counter and went straight to my room to put on my jammies. TV, that was what I needed, anything to stop myself from thinking about Jason, or Bruce, or how we needed to hurry and close this case.

I'd just sat down when there was a knock on my door. Tuesday was still out of town on a modeling gig, and I didn't know anyone else who would stop by my house after nine. Or anytime really. I pushed that depressing thought out of my mind and got up to answer. A quick check of the peephole told me Jason still hadn't gotten over his snit.

"Hey."

"May I come in?"

"It depends."

"On what?" His lip twitched. He sure was handsome when he smiled but he wouldn't be doing it for long.

"On why you're here and if you're finally gonna stop giving me motion sickness."

"I'm here to apologize."

"Then, no, you can't come in. I'll see you tomorrow."

"Wait. What?" His hand shot out and he stopped me from closing the door.

"I don't want an apology, Jason. I want the why."

"The why?"

"Yes. Why are you so hot and cold with me? Why one minute you're smiling at me and the next scowling? Then there's today. So, if you're ready to talk about those things, come on in. If you just want to say you're sorry, save it."

"You're so fucking different from her."

"What?" My lungs filled to capacity as I sucked in

a breath. Was he comparing me to Kayla? That stung, bad.

"You drive me crazy."

"Back atcha, Jason."

I opened the door and let him in. I had no idea what he wanted to get off his chest, but if he was in the mood to talk, I'd lend an ear.

9

SOMETHING DEEP HAD BEEN BREWING over the last few weeks. I couldn't place the feeling but then that wasn't surprising. I'd spent the last two years trying to feel nothing at all, so when all of these emotions started firing off, I didn't know what to do with them. Today, when Bruce had asked her out, I could no longer deny I felt something. I'd done pretty much the worst thing I could've done and kissed her.

I gave in to temptation, and the moment I touched her, insane desire mixed with guilt. I'd never wanted to be with another woman other than my wife, even after our marriage was over. Even after Kayla had died, I still hadn't dared look at another woman, not until Mercy.

After I'd kissed her, I left the office and spent hours driving around trying to get my shit together. But now that I'd managed to crack the door open, I didn't know how to shut it. I ended up pulling into Mercy's driveway and, before I knew what I was doing, I knocked on her door. Maybe I wanted her to slam it in my face. Tell me to fuck off and that I was a bastard for touching her. Hell, I didn't know.

Now that I was inside, I didn't know where to begin or what to say.

"I'm a goddamn mess," I admitted.

"You are," she readily agreed.

Her answer was so typical of her, I lost it and laughed to near hysteria. Leave it to Mercy to agree.

"I can't stop thinking about you." I moved toward her, and she made no effort to back up. "I tried. I really fucking tried to stay away from you."

"Why?"

"Because I don't want to hurt you."

She was right there inches away from me. My hands ached to touch her.

"You won't."

I needed her to tell me to back off, to stop, something. I wasn't strong enough to stay away. Everything about Mercy called to every part of me. Even the parts of me I'd thought would be cold and dead forever.

This time, she moved. Her hands went to the back of my head to pull me forward as she came up on her toes. She pressed her lips against mine, and every nerve ending in my body began to spark. She yanked my shirt up, and I bent forward so she could pull it off. Hers was suddenly off and tossed aside, and her lips were on mine. Within minutes the rest of our clothes were torn off, and I picked her up. Her back hit the wall behind us. Mercy's strong legs wrapped around my waist, her naked body pressed against mine was almost too much to take. Both of us were in a frenzy to touch and taste. Her tongue glided against mine, and I couldn't remember anything that tasted better—ever. In a smooth, hard thrust I was inside of her, wetness and heat enveloped my dick, causing my eyes to roll to the back of my head. Jesus. Not a word was spoken as I pumped into her welcoming body. She rocked against me, perfectly in sync. Her hands in my hair yanked, and it spurred me on. Standing in Mercy's living room, up against the wall, I fucked her like she was the first breath of fresh air I'd had in years. And, in a way, she was.

"Jason," she moaned. "God, yes!"

Her head hit the wall, and my mouth chased after hers. I needed her lips on mine, I had to taste the excitement on her tongue. My balls drew up tight, and heat tingled my spine. Her pussy convulsed and spasmed around my dick, and there wasn't a damn thing I could do to stop the come from exploding out of me. With one more thrust I stayed planted as deep as I could and savored the sensation. The last bit of my orgasm spilled into her, and guilt consumed me. It overtook every ounce of pleasure I'd felt moments before and stole away the peace Mercy had provided.

What the fuck did I do?

Mercy's lips were on my neck, and she slowly pulled back but before she could look at me, I closed my eyes.

"Don't you dare shut down on me, Jason Walker."

When I didn't answer she unlocked her legs from around my hips and wiggled until I set her on her feet. Both of us stood butt-assed naked, nowhere to go, nothing to hide behind.

"Follow me." She grabbed my hand, giving me no choice but to follow or yank my hand free. I was too overcome with emotion to do anything but trail behind her. Like the lost fucking puppy I was. When had I turned into such a pansy-assed idiot?

When we reached her bedroom, she flipped on the lamp on her nightstand. I was grateful it was dim, the last thing I wanted her to see was my shame. She climbed onto her bed and pulled me next to her. We laid in silence for a long time. My thoughts were all over the place. Torn down the middle. Kayla was dead, had been for a long time, but a nagging voice told me

I'd cheated. But worse than that, I'd just had the single most passionate sexual experience of my life. Mercy was so full of life, she was this force of nature that drew me in. I wanted more of her. More of what we just had against the wall, more of her in my arms, more of the confusion she caused.

10

GOOD GOD, I was sore in all the right places. Never had I been taken so completely. And by completely, I mean when Jason was moving inside of me nothing else had existed. He was all I could feel. My brain had shut off and lust had taken over. But when the passion waned, and reality crept back in, Jason had shut down faster than I'd thought possible. Oh, I'd known he was going to pull away. I'd just figured it would take an hour. I hadn't imagined it would be immediately.

Jason shifted and pulled me closer to him, forcing me to move my arm or it would be squished. With no other place to put it, I draped it over his stomach. I was statue still, waiting for him to make the next move. I'd taken us this far, it was up to him where we went next. If he wanted to get up and leave, I wouldn't ask him to stay. I also wouldn't blame him. But whatever it was, the choice was his.

I hadn't realized I was holding my breath until he laced his fingers with mine, and his other hand started moving over my hip. It was then I finally exhaled.

"Thank you for understanding."

"You're welcome."

"You're the first woman I've had sex with in about six or seven years." Seven years? That didn't make any sense, his wife had only passed away two years ago. "I guess you were right, it was just like riding a bike." Thankfully his body was shaking under mine when the laughter I was holding back broke free. "Though, I think mostly it was because it was you. There's something about you that makes me insane."

I wasn't touching any of what he'd just said with a ten-foot pole. I had a way with words, and not a good way. It was best I stayed silent. His hand kept gliding over my hip, and the wetness between my legs had nothing to do with our previous encounter. I glanced down the muscular plane of his stomach and was happy to see an erection. I tilted my head back so I could see him and was pleased when I saw a smile.

"You're so beautiful," he said.

"You're not bad yourself, hot stuff."

That was an understatement. He was super

fucking hot. His blue eyes were so incredible they made you want to stare at them for hours. And while his hair wasn't as black as his sister's it was pretty close. Darker than dark brown, but not jet-black. He kept it short on the sides but long enough on top you wanted to run your fingers through it.

"I want to touch you, Mercy."

"You don't need to ask."

He unlaced our fingers and gently traced around my areola before plucking my nipple to a hard peak. He couldn't reach my other one as it was pressed against his side, so he moved lower down my stomach, not stopping until he ran his finger between my lips, gathering wetness and pulling it back up to my clit. Just as my body started to tingle, he stopped. I wanted to cry out, however my protest died when he dipped his fingertip inside of me. My hips came off the bed, wanting him deeper, but he pulled back, not allowing me to spear myself the way I wanted to. Over and over he tortured me, circling my clit then back down only pressing in the tip of his finger.

"Climb on top of me, I want to watch while you fuck me."

He didn't need to ask me twice. I mounted up like a cowgirl ready to win the blue ribbon. My very unsexy move earned me a pussy-clenching smile, and my heart swelled.

With both of his hands on my ass, squeezing my cheeks, he said, "Lean forward. I want to taste your nipples but damn if I can't take my hands off your ass to grab one."

I did as he asked, and when his lips wrapped around my nipple, he wasn't gentle. He sucked and nibbled one before he went to the other, and with just as much force he pulled it into his mouth. I couldn't tear my eyes away from the sexy scene. Holy shit, it was so hot seeing him abuse my sensitive breasts, I wondered if I could orgasm just from watching.

One of his hands came off my ass, and I could feel the head of his dick rubbing my clit before it was pressed against my opening. All I needed to do was slide down. I didn't know what I was waiting for, but when Jason popped my nipple out of his mouth, and his eyes locked with mine, I was happy as hell I hadn't just slammed down. I would've missed the best part.

On a slow glide down, I took his dick inch by inch. Jason's mouth opened slightly, and his blue irises darkened.

"Mercy," he panted. "You feel so goddamn good." I had to agree, it was good. Better than good. It was fantastic. I was fully seated on his lap, with his dick so deep it was nearly painful. My hands roamed over his chest, touching every part of him I could. I still hadn't looked away. I was too mesmerized by the look of wonderment in his eyes. "Fuck me."

I leaned forward to kiss him, and my sensitized clit rubbed against his pubic hair, and I nearly lost my balance. Luckily his grip on my hips kept me in place. His fingertips dug in, and I hoped there was a mark. I wanted to look in the mirror tomorrow and see where his strong hands had guided me up and down his dick.

My lips were still a few millimeters away from his when he whispered, "Kiss me."

"You're bossy," I muttered back.

"You ain't seen bossy yet."

He didn't wait for me to lean in, he lifted his head and took what he wanted.

I learned something about passion that night with Jason. When two people have an undeniable attraction, the longer the allure is denied, the more the lust and desire build. When the need to touch and feel the other person finally erupts, it's out of this world.

Everything was escalating at once. His tongue dueled with mine, his hands kneaded my ass, and I rocked up and down on his dick as fast and hard as I could. I was one big ball of sensation. I was trying to hold back my orgasm until he went.

"Please hurry, Jason."

"Don't wait for me, Mercy, come."

"I can't. I won't be able to move once I do."

"Let. Go." I couldn't hold it back when he thrust up.

He remained still for a moment and let me catch my breath before he rolled me over, pulled out, and rolled me again to my stomach.

"Up on your knees."

He tugged my hips until I was where he wanted me, then he slammed back inside. With a handful of my hair, he tugged, making me look over my shoulder.

"You are so goddamn sexy, Mercy, I can't stand it. I want to touch you everywhere. I want to lick and taste every inch of you from your sweet mouth to your tight pussy." His hard, fast thrusts were stealing my breath. "I want to fuck you in every way possible." His rhythm started to falter. "You feel so fucking good I'm gonna come."

He let go of my hair and grabbed both of my hips before he shoved all the way in and roared his release. His come spilled out of my pussy and dripped down my thighs. Good Lord, I'd never thought I'd like a man talking dirty to me, but when Jason did it, it was hot as hell.

I waited for him to pull out before I went flat on my stomach. This time instead of pulling away, his hands rubbed over the back of my calves and thighs. I wiggled when he traced my ass crack, all the way up my back. He kissed my shoulder blade before he whispered, "You are seriously one sexy, beautiful woman. And you have the finest ass I've ever seen. I could spend an entire afternoon worshiping the beauty that is your ass."

"Years of Pringles chips have given me that ass."

"Baby, tomorrow I'm buying you a lifetime supply."

He rolled next to me and pulled me back to his side like we'd been lying before round two. The cool air of the room hit my fevered skin, and I shivered. Without asking, he knifed up yanking the blankets out from under me and covered us both up. Once we were situated, I was nice and comfy and ready for sleep.

"I didn't use a condom."

"I know. I'm on birth control." I was going to leave it at that until I remembered he'd shared a bit of personal information with me earlier. "I haven't had sex in about three years. I've been tested since then."

He gave no indication he'd heard me, but I knew he was awake because his hand was still moving over my ass. Guess he was telling the truth when he'd said he liked it.

"You staying over?" I tried to keep my voice even, not wanting to convey my preference.

"Is that all right with you?"

"Yeah. Whatever you want." Was what I said. Inside I was doing summersaults and jumping jacks.

I cuddled in closer and was almost asleep when I heard him whisper, "Mercy, Mercy, Mercy, you make me lose my mind."

11

SOMETHING heavy and hot was draped over me, pulling me from my sleep, and a tiny hand was covering my heart. I opened my eyes and was startled when long, brown hair framed a beautiful face, not short, blonde.

Then I remembered.

Mercy.

I glanced at the clock on the nightstand—five a.m. I'd slept through the night with no nightmares. Not a single dream about my old life. That hadn't happened in years. Mercy stirred and she mewed in her sleep, bringing back memories from the night before. I hadn't come over here with the intention of fucking her, and certainly not twice, or to spend the night. Damn, I'm an asshole. What now? I'd never done the morning after. Did I wait until she was awake? Stay for breakfast? Wake her and go for round three?

There were too many conflicting emotions swirling in my head. Excitement and shame. Embarrassment and anticipation. I'd admitted I hadn't had sex in a very long time, and Mercy didn't bat an eye or question it. Maybe she hadn't believed me, but didn't want to call me out on it. It was true. The first three years Kayla and I were married were good. In the beginning we couldn't keep our hands off each other. It was never wild, never rip each other's clothes off passionate. It was sweet and gentle. *She* was sweet and gentle. Kind and soft-hearted. I'd never spoken to her the way I did Mercy. I never felt a soul-deep need to fuck her senseless. Guilt slammed into my chest as I compared the two. But there it was—the truth. Kayla had been my best friend, my past, my advisor, she'd been comfortable. And I'd been those things to her.

I'd also been her caretaker. After she'd gotten sick, our only focus was her getting better. Doctors, chemo, radiation. Together we fought to get her well. She'd lay in my arms at night, and we'd talk, our friendship growing deeper, but our relationship morphed. Somewhere along the line we'd stopped being husband and wife and had gone back to just being friends. The best of friends. After she'd gotten better, we'd tried to rekindle our sexual relationship, but neither of us were into it. It was unspoken, but she'd no longer touched me or even kissed me more than a peck. There'd been no one else. That wasn't Kayla's style. We'd lived happily together as roommates. Pretending to the outside world we were still happily married. When in reality—we were not.

Maybe my best option was to sneak out while Mercy was still sleeping to avoid any awkwardness. I could get up, go home, and kick my own ass for being such an asshole. That was probably my best option. But I couldn't force myself to move. She felt too good pressed against me. Her hand on my heart seemed to be the only thing stopping it from pounding out of my chest. The gut-wrenching dread of starting a new day was noticeably absent. The lethargy I'd had when I opened my eyes was gone. It was so wrong. Wrong on so many levels. She deserved so much better than me. I wasn't just bent, I was broken. I had nothing to offer her, but the thought of not seeing her tore me to shreds. Now that I'd been in her bed was it possible to go back?

The alarm clock buzzed, and Mercy stirred. Sitting up she blinked a few times before reaching over me to hit the snooze button.

"Six already?" Six? Dear God, I'd been lying awake in bed for an hour? "Morning."

It was hard to think, let alone speak, when her perky, full breasts swayed in front of my face as she moved across me to lay back down. My dick throbbed, and I knew it was time to get out of her bed before I lost control again.

"Morning," I croaked out.

Mercy's dainty hand trailed up and down my stomach, which did nothing to calm my dick or my rioting emotions. Her touch was magic, it could excite and calm me at the same time. All thoughts of my past life flew out the window, all the reasons we shouldn't be in bed together no longer mattered. A simple touch of her fingertips made me want to fuck the hell out of her. I didn't want gentle, I wanted wild, pulse pounding, dirty sex. Deep needs within me I'd never allowed to surface. I wanted to control her orgasms, make her chant my name, beg me to please her.

"Take a shower with me before you go?"

I nodded my answer and tapped her ass. She didn't roll off the other side of the bed, instead she crawled on top of me and paused. She looked so goddamn hot perched up there. Rosy nipples tipped the sexiest pair of tits I'd ever seen. She was strong and lean, so fucking beautiful. My dick was trapped between us, nestled between her pussy lips. Mercy rocked and her wetness coated my erection.

"Shower," I growled.

I needed her bent over, her tight, firm ass filling my vision as my dick tunneled in and out of her. I wanted to smack it and see my handprint welt as her pussy tightened around me. By the time I'd gotten myself under control, pushing aside thoughts of spanking her, she'd already turned on the shower.

Cock in hand I stepped into the shower. Mercy's gaze dropped from my face to where I was stroking my shaft.

"Is this what you wanted?" I continued to jerk my dick, pre-come beading on the tip.

Mercy licked her lips, and I wondered what her mouth would feel like. Would she be timid and shy or would she be enthusiastic? I bet she'd suck me with the same vigor as she lived her life.

"Yes."

"Turn around, hands on the wall." Her eyes flared, and her lips quirked.

"Damn, you're hot when you're bossy."

"Pleased you think so."

She turned to face the wall, and my gaze ate up every inch of her. "So fucking hot. You ready for me?"

"Yes."

My hand went between her legs, happy when my fingers were coated in her excitement. I lined my dick up and leaned forward, kissing her shoulder and neck before licking her earlobe. Mercy's head fell to the side and her ass pushed back.

"Brace yourself, baby, I'm gonna fuck the hell out of you until we're both screaming out in pleasure."

"Do it, Jason, Fuck me—"

I slammed into her, cutting off any further instructions.

She chanted my name, prayed to God, and begged me not to stop. Her filthy pleas spurred me on. My need built, and lust took over. But something else happened, something bigger, something that scared the hell out of me—I was falling for her. There was no denying it. The thought should've made my dick shrivel, but, instead, it swelled. We finished in a hot explosion of expletives and bliss. But more than that, something that felt eerily like happiness took root.

12

OKAY, so, I slept with Jason. Not once, but three mind-bending times. We were adults, we could work together and not let things get weird. I hoped.

Thankfully I worked in a place where jeans and sneakers were acceptable, because after our shower this morning my legs were still jelly. And I hadn't had to do anything but stand there. Jason did all the work. However, it didn't matter if he was the one doing the thrusting, sex with Jason was a full-body experience. Every muscle in my body still felt him.

Now I was sitting at my desk, trying to work, but the butterflies in my stomach were preventing me from concentrating on my inbox. I couldn't stop wondering if Jason would come upstairs and work in my office, and, if not, would he come up to say hello? Would he ignore me or smile or wink or acknowledge me in any way? I was pathetic and sounded like a silly, love-sick girl instead of a grown woman.

Wait! I wasn't love-sick, was I? Three rounds of the best-sex-ever couldn't make a sane woman fall in love, could it? No. It was lust. The on again off again crush I'd had was now infused with a heavy dose of desire. That was all. I knew better than to fall for Jason. Sex. That was all it was. And if I wanted to keep having it with him, I'd better keep my feelings for him in check. It's not like I've never had a friends with benefits arrangement before. I didn't have a problem keeping my emotions out of it. But then I'd never spent the night or showered or felt any type of connection to anyone before either.

I junked all the crap I'd been cc'd on that was unimportant and read Bruce's last message. His team didn't think it was worth it to try and track down a solvent that was unregulated and easily purchased. They didn't want to waste valuable resources. He'd also run the Stevenses credit cards and Delaney was right, they'd been out of town in Savannah. He was going back to their house today. My gut told me it was going to be a dead end. I didn't think Mary Beth was manufacturing or selling anything. Her house was simply a party house due to lack of parental supervision.

My office phone rang and, without looking away from my monitor, I hit the speaker button to answer.

"Mercy James."

"Hi, Mercy. It's Delaney Walker. Jason's sister."

"Yeah. Hi. Everything okay?"

"I think so. Listen, I'm sorry to bother you, but Jason's not answering his phone and not returning my texts. Which, the calls, I understand, but I texted him I had something important to tell him and still nothing. Is he okay? He didn't answer his office line either."

"Yeah, I think so, he was fine this morning."

"Oh, good, so he's at work?"

"Um." Before I could answer Delaney, my office door opened and Jason walked in carrying two cups of coffee. "Hey, your sister's trying to get ahold of you. You're not answering your cell."

"I left it at your house this morning." I waved my hand frantically trying to get him to stop speaking but it was too late. "Guess I wasn't thinking about my phone after—"

"Delaney's on the phone," I all but shouted and pointed to my desk.

"Hey, big brother." Delaney chuckled.

Jason stood stock-still. His body so tight I was afraid he was going to shatter if I breathed in his direction.

"Not a word to anyone," he growled.

"Mums the word."

"I'm serious, Delaney. I've kept your secret about Carter for the last eight years."

"Take it easy. I told you I wouldn't say anything and I won't. You don't need to threaten me. I get it."

"Sorry. I know you do." Jason relaxed a fraction now that he had his sister's promise not to tell anyone he'd been at my house.

I can't say him wanting to keep me a secret didn't hurt, it did. I could understand why, but it still stung. Neither of us were doing anything wrong. We were both single adults and could spend time with anyone we wanted. Which meant it was me, specifically, he didn't want anyone to know about. Maybe it was good timing, having the reminder we were nothing but friends who'd had sex. It didn't matter how much chemistry there was between us, how the sparks ignited, how the sex had been wild and awe-inspiring. He didn't now, and would never, see me as anything more than a quick and dirty fuck. Which I wasn't opposed to, I just needed to keep my wits about me.

"Everything okay?" Jason asked his sister.

"I'm fine. You asked me to keep my ear to the ground so I poked around a little."

"Delaney! I didn't ask you to poke around."

"Sheesh. I know you didn't. But I was thinking about something. Last year a new science teacher transferred to Parkside. The science club's numbers went up a little last year, but this year they've almost doubled."

"Okay. So she's a good teacher? Aren't schools really pushing STEM now?"

"He. The teacher is a man. He's my age and good looking. Maybe it's nothing and the girls are joining the club because they want to flirt with him. I looked at his schedule, and he teaches AP Chem."

"Was Nessa in his class?"

"No, only juniors and seniors, but there's a Jeff White in his AP Chem class. And Nessa and Jeff are both in the science club. I checked the calendar and twice a week they meet at lunch and every other week after school for two hours."

"What's his name?" I asked.

"Derek Lowe. Do you want—"

"No. I don't want you to do anything more. As a matter of fact, stay away from him until we run him."

"Fine. But you know I can help you."

"You will be helping by staying out of it. I can't concentrate on my job if I'm worried about you."

"Are you coming to Sunday dinner?"

"Delaney—"

"You should bring Mercy. Just saying. Love you,

big brother, have to run. Talk to you later." Delaney had spoken so quickly her words had run together. She also, smartly, hung up before Jason could scold her about mentioning dinner—again.

"I'm so sorry," I started. "I should've started with, she was on the phone."

"It's fine. She won't say anything. She has a secret the size of Hiroshima she doesn't want getting out."

Bam—direct hit. He didn't say he didn't care if she told his family, just that he had enough blackmail material to keep her quiet.

"Who's Carter?"

"The man she's been in love with since she was old enough to recognize the emotion."

"And . . . that's a big secret because?"

Jason settled into the chair in front of me and stretched out his long legs. "Because we grew up with him. My dad has three best friends, they were in the Army together, and when they retired the four of them went into the security contracting business. Anyway, Clark, Lenox, and Levi are their names. They may not be our blood, but we've always called them "uncle." We grew up with their kids, and when I say grew up, I mean, we're a close family. We did everything together. It was like each of us had four sets of parents and ten siblings. Carter Lenox is my Uncle Lenox and Aunt Lily's oldest son."

"But not really your aunt and uncle so Delaney and Carter are not really cousins?"

"Correct. Carter is hung up on a few things. He's three years older than her, he doesn't think the family will approve, and his job is dangerous."

"Does he know how she feels?"

"The two of them have been sneaking around since she was seventeen and Carter came home on leave from the Naval Academy."

"So he was twenty?"

"And now you see the issue. It took a lot not to kick his ass after I found out. Delaney's my sister and Carter's one of my closest friends. The only thing that stopped me was he was begging me for the beating. He rambled on about how much he loved her, how it was wrong, how he deserved for me to hurt him. He was a wreck. In the end, I couldn't touch him. I feel sorry for him. He loves my sister more than anything in this world but he won't be with her."

"Wow, that's really sad. So that's it? They love each other from a distance."

"Pretty much. He's in the Navy, when he comes into town, they hook up, he leaves, my sister crumbles, and waits for the next visit."

"What the fuck? She needs to kick his ass to the curb. Delaney is gorgeous and should not be waiting around for any man."

Jason's deep rumbling laughter filled my office and I didn't know what was funny but I was enjoying the sound. I needed to savor every laugh, every smile, every minute I had with him. Something in the back of my mind told me this was only temporary and it would be gone soon. I needed to soak up and enjoy everything I could, because when he was gone it was going to hurt like a bitch.

"Damn, I love it when you get fierce and protective. Normally, I would agree with you. But Delaney is not the only one who's left devastated. His team nicknamed him monk. Never, not once, has he taken a woman while he's been away from Delaney. And they are not together. No promises have been made and no claims to be faithful. My sister's it for him, there will never be anyone else. All they need to do is work their shit out, but I don't see that happening for a while. Something earth-shattering would have to happen before Carter Lenox pulls his head out of his ass. He is as stubborn as they come."

"Oh, so, it's a family trait," I muttered.

"What?"

"Nothing. Bruce sent us an email . . ."

I steered the conversation to work, not wanting to think about poor Delaney's love life. I seemed to be in the same situation she was in, minus the love, and the life-long friends part. It seemed we both wanted men we couldn't have. Maybe I hadn't gotten over my need to fix people as much as I thought I had. Red lights were flashing and sirens were blaring, warning me to pull back. But I knew the next time Jason came to me, I'd welcome him.

13

I'D BEEN TOSSING my phone back and forth in my hands for the last thirty minutes. Dreading the call I needed to make. It was long overdue, and I was going to catch shit for it.

Man the fuck up, Walker.

I dialed the number I knew by heart, and it rang twice before the call connected.

"Hey, Bud, how's it goin'?"

"Hey, Dad."

Suddenly I wasn't sure what I wanted to say. That's not true. I knew, I just didn't know how to say it.

"Delaney said she saw you the other day. Something about a case you're working on spilling over into her school. Anything we should know?"

"One of her students OD'd. The investigation actually started at Polytech. We caught word they have a pharma issue over there. Local PD put together a task force and asked for our help. Seems we've stepped into something else."

"Not your usual assignment," he noted.

"Not even a little bit. A DI agent asked me to work the case with Diversion Control."

"Mercy James?"

Shit, goddamn, of course my dad would know. All it would've taken was Delaney telling him I'd shown up with Mercy, and my dad would have had all the intel on her within minutes.

"Yep. How far did you dig?"

The answering chuckle told me I was right. I should be offended or at least annoyed, but I knew why my dad did it. His time as Army Special Forces left him mostly distrusting.

"Not as far as I go with your sisters. Shame what happened to her dad and brother."

"Hate to tell you, Pop, but you looked up the wrong Mercy James. She doesn't have a brother."

I remembered the conversation. The first time we'd exchanged anything personal, I'd asked her if she had any siblings after I'd told her about my sisters. She'd said no, then went on to tell me her mom had died. I still couldn't wrap my head around what it would've been like to grow up without a mother. My mom was such an important part of my family, we'd be lost if we didn't have her.

"She may not have a brother now, but she did. He died at eighteen, drug overdose. A few years later her dad, Officer Paul James, died in the line of duty. Ironically, he worked on the guns and drugs task force. Good cop according to his sheet."

"She fucking lied to me."

"Come again?"

"I told her about Delaney, Quinn, Hadley, and Adalynn. When I asked her if she had any siblings, she said no."

"Son, you should understand that sometimes—"

"No, Dad, she told me about her mom dying in childbirth. Told me her dad was a cop. She even compared herself to Quinn. But she never mentioned a brother or her father dying. She told me he'd been strict, didn't want her going into law enforcement, and he never got over his wife's death."

A few things occurred to me after I'd repeated the conversation back to my dad. Was Mercy comparing me to her father? She'd said he was lonely, didn't date, never remarried, and couldn't get over her mom dying. Is that what she thought about me? I couldn't get over *my* wife's death? She thought I was some lonely sap? I also couldn't believe she'd lied to me. Flat out didn't tell me the truth.

"I gotta go."

"Jason! Bud, I'm gonna caution you from going to her and saying something you'll regret."

"What makes you think I'll regret it? I talked to her about Quinn. I told her about my sisters. Personal—"

"Son, telling a woman about your sisters is not personal. It is a normal friendly conversation. And I know you'll regret anything you say in anger—because you're angry."

"That makes no fucking sense."

"When was the last time you cared about *anything* enough to get angry?" Well, fuck. Nothing slipped by Jasper Walker. I shouldn't have called him. He was too perceptive. I never could hide anything from my dad. "Right. Now when was the last time you cared enough about a *woman* or what she did or didn't say to get angry?"

"It's not like that."

Or was it? Shit, I didn't know what it was like.

"I'm not asking what anything is like. I'm pleased as fuck you're feeling something, even if it's anger. Because, Bud, I gotta tell you, you numb is excruciating to watch. All I'm saying is check yourself before you put Mercy on blast. She may have her reasons for not wanting to talk about her brother and dad, the same way you don't want to talk about Kayla."

"Yeah, all right."

"You're not gonna listen to me, are you?"

"I listened, I just don't know if I can take your advice."

"Your mom would like to see you. If you don't want to come to Sunday dinner, I suggest you call her and make arrangements for another night of the week. You should do that soon. And you should also consider having Mercy sitting next to your ass at your mom's table one night soon, too."

"It really isn't like *that*. It's not a bring home to meet the family situation." I cringed saying the words out loud. What kind of prick was I to admit that to my dad? Mercy was not some bar pickup. I had no right treating her like she was.

"Once upon a time I knew a young man that was dumb enough to think the same thing. Unfortunately or fortunately for you, depending on how you look at it, there is nothing you can tell me that I haven't walked through. Think back over your life, and what you know about me, your mom, and how we started. Then you think on your life and how we've walked the same path. Reach out, Bud, that's all you need to do. We're waiting."

"I miss the good old days. When I was a kid and all there was to worry about was whether Delaney was going to go into my room and mess up my video games."

Damn, life was easy then. I'd damn near give anything to go back there.

"Son, these are the good old days. Today, right now. You're wasting them. It's time to wake the fuck up and start living. You're still alive, start acting like it."

With that sucker punch to the gut, my dad disconnected. He was right, I was alive, I just didn't know how to start living again.

Within minutes, I was in my car on the way to Mercy's house. A smarter man would've heeded my dad's advice and cooled off first. But no one had ever accused me of being smart, then there was the fact that Mercy drove me to stupidity. I lost my mind when I thought about her. Completely and totally dumb when it came to her.

I pulled into her driveway and hoped she wasn't home. Now that I was there, I knew it was a bad idea but I couldn't stop myself from stomping to the door and knocking. When she answered with a smile, I pushed my way past her and, without so much as a hello, started in, and I was brutal.

"So, why don't we start with your brother and dad, then we'll talk about why you lied to me."

I watched in morbid fascination as her face went from sheet white to bright red.

"Excuse me?"

"You heard me. Your brother and your dad?"

"What about them?" she growled.

Yeah, she was pissed now, but I was furious so we were almost even.

"I thought you said you didn't have any siblings?"

"I don't, he's dead."

"Why didn't you just say that?"

"Oh, I don't know, let me think. That's right, because when you asked, you were giving me whiplash with your hot and cold shit. Kinda like you are now. Need another reason? It's probably the same reason why you don't talk about Kayla."

"What about her? There's nothing to tell."

"There's plenty to tell but you keep it locked up so tight I don't think you know where you've hidden the key."

"I married Kayla when I was twenty-one. She was twenty-three the first time she got cancer. She beat it the first time. It came back when she was twenty-eight and that time it was more aggressive, and she decided she didn't want to go through treatment again. She was dead in six months. That's it. End of story."

Cancer. Six goddamn letters that had blown my life up. It was easier to say the words in anger. Easier to spit out the facts when there were no other emotions involved, when I could keep the crushing pain of her death pushed down deep.

"How'd you feel about her refusing treatment the second time?"

"Doesn't matter what I felt. It was her decision."

"I didn't ask that. I asked how you felt about it."

"I fucking hated it. I was furious with her. I wanted her to try again, and she flat out refused!" I yelled. My hands scrubbed over my face. This was a bad idea. "I can't do this."

"Can't or won't?" she pushed.

"You have no idea—"

"I don't? My older brother got involved in drugs when we were in high school, he was a senior. My dad was on an overnight shift, and my brother stumbled in around four a.m. and woke me up. I went into the living room to find him convulsing. I called nine-one-one but he was dead before they arrived. Tox came back, he had enough tranquilizers in his system to take down a fucking moose. My dad shut down even more after that. He was reckless at work and was hellbent on finding those responsible for selling my brother the drugs. It took almost four years but when there was a string of deaths in the area all with the same cocktail of drugs my brother died from, he went in to make the bust. He knew going in he wasn't coming home and he went in anyway. I was twenty, and my dad made the decision to leave me an orphan. So, Jason, you see, I understand. The difference is, you wake up every morning and decide to let the past dictate your future. I wake up and I'm thrilled for a new day."

"She was divorcing me!" I bellowed. "Before she got the second diagnosis. She had the separation agreement drawn up and had signed it. Every fucking morning, I look at her pretty, flowing signature on that paper and think, even her damn name looked happy to be leaving me."

"Why in the hell do you still have those papers? And why would you look at them?"

"To remind me what a bad husband I was."

"Throw them away, Jason."

It wouldn't matter if I did, I had the agreement memorized. I knew every detail she'd had typed up. It was an easy separation. A no fault divorce with no support. She wanted nothing from me. Just a fresh start and the opportunity to be happy.

"You know the worst part? The part that's unforgivable?"

"I don't think anything you could've done was unforgiveable."

She had no idea what a dick I was. How many times had I sat next to my sick wife and beat myself up for not being a better man? The type of man she deserved by her side.

"I didn't love her," I rushed out. I'd never admitted that to anyone but Kayla. The words tasted like shit as I said them, and I was afraid I was going to choke on the guilt and pain. "Not the way a man is supposed to love his wife. We had three good years together. Then she got sick."

"Jason—"

How the fuck had me coming over here turned into this? All I wanted to know was why she'd lied to me and there I was spilling my fucking guts about stuff I didn't want to talk about, didn't want to think about.

"So there you have it. You know everything. We were roommates. Nothing more. We didn't have sex, we didn't kiss. We shared a platonic bed. She died in my arms making me promise I'd move on and find someone to love. How in the fuck am I supposed to do that when she never got to find a real man to love her the way she needed to be loved? She never found passion, or soul deep hunger. All she got was me."

I'd laid my shit bare, opened a vein and was hemorrhaging. Everything I'd never wanted to admit lingered in the air, threatening to suffocate me. She deserved more, hell, both of them did. Mercy and Kayla. I'd ruined Kayla's life but I wouldn't let myself ruin Mercy's.

"I need to leave."

"DON'T you dare walk out on me, Jason."

His chest was heaving like he'd run a marathon, sucking all the oxygen out of the room. There was so much information to process, and I wasn't sure how he'd found out about my dad and PJ, but all of that could wait. But Jason couldn't. Not when he looked like he was ready to crawl out of his skin.

"Why the hell would you want me to stay? Didn't you hear me?"

"I did. Heard every word."

Knowing he and Kayla were separating before her cancer came back shone a new light on the situation. I now understood where his guilt came from. Something I could never understand before. It wasn't his fault she got sick, and certainly not his fault when she didn't want treatment. I didn't blame her for not wanting to spend the last months she had left going to doctors' visits and sick as a dog. I wouldn't either, not that I would tell him that right now.

"I need to leave."

"No. You need to come lie down with me."

"What?"

"I'm serious. You need to calm down before you decide to drive anywhere."

"I'm fine. I shouldn't have come here."

He started for the door, but I darted across the room and got there faster.

"You're not leaving while you're upset. No way." With eyes as big as saucers he reached for the door. "I'm not kidding."

"And what, Mercy, you're going to stop me?"

"Damn right, I am."

We stood staring at each other in the world's longest Mexican standoff. Some crazy arcs of electricity zapped between us. He was pissed. I was pissed. Emotions were high, and he looked crazy sexy.

"I need you to stay."

"I can't. Not the way I'm feeling. I have to leave."

We were back to watching one another. Silently waiting for the other to break. I wasn't moving from in front of the door, and he wanted out. If I hadn't known what it had taken for Jason to share what he did, and he wasn't looking at me like I was his last hope for survival, I would've moved. But I did and he was. There was no mistaking the hunger swirling in his eyes.

"I'm afraid I won't be able to stop if I stay," he damn near whispered. "And I don't want to hurt you."

"I don't want you to stop."

"You don't get it. I'm falling for you. I think about you all the damn time. I want you more than I've ever wanted a woman. I want you to feel the depth of my pain and guilt. I want you to take it and understand it. I want you to fucking see me. This me, the broken man, and still want me just as badly as I want you. I want everything, but I have nothing to give you in return. I'll wreck you. And, one day, when you look at me with devastation marring your beautiful face, you'll hate me for what I've done to your life."

"I won't let you. You'll never have the power to destroy me."

"But I want that power, Mercy. I want you to fall in love with me. I don't want to be alone in what I feel for you."

Christ Almighty, he was killing me. I wanted to believe what he was telling me but I was afraid. He was emotional and had just unloaded a heavy burden.

"You won't be alone. I'll give you everything you need. All of what you want. But you need to under-stand, no one will ever have the power to crush me. It won't matter how much I love you, how badly I want you. You have to know, at the end of the day, if you leave me, I will push through it. And that does not mean I won't give myself to you completely. Because I will."

"I'm fucked up, Mercy."

"Aren't we all?"

Some of the hurt had crept out of his eyes, but none of the need or lust had waned. When he looked at me like I was the next meal he wanted to devour, I felt strong and brave and wanted. I would give him every-thing I had to give but I'd promised myself a long time ago that no matter what happened in my life I would never break. Not when PJ died, not when my dad left me, not when I had to power through shit at work. I was stronger than that.

"Take what you need, Jason."

"I can't. I'm too afraid to touch you."

"Take. It."

"I can't be gentle."

"I don't want gentle. Gentle is not us. I want you to rip my clothes from my body and take what you need. Because whatever it is you take, will be exactly what I want to give."

It didn't take Jason but a moment to have my clothes in a heap on the floor and his soon followed. And true to what he'd said he hadn't been gentle. He lifted me up, carried me to my bedroom, deposited me on the bed, and loomed over me, looking unsure.

"Take it, Jason." His arms trembled, and his breathing was labored. He began to shake his head, and I made the decision for us. "Fine. I'll take it."

I bucked my hips, forcing him to his back, and rolled on top of him. I didn't waste anytime, not when I knew what I wanted and what he needed to calm his mind. I took his long, thick dick in my hand and stroked his already erect shaft. His hips flexed, and he thrusted up into my hand.

"Harder, Mercy."

I tightened my grip and pumped faster, using my other hand I reached down and cupped his balls and rolled them. His eyes closed, and his back arched.

"Jesus!"

Pre-come was leaking and if it wasn't physically impossible for me to reach, I would've licked the salty fluid. I wanted to know what he tasted like, what he felt like in my mouth. Another time. Right now, I needed Jason on the brink. I needed him only thinking about us, and how good my hands felt.

"Enough. Fuck me."

I lined the tip of his dick up and slammed down.

"Good God!"

He could say that again. He stretched me to full. My nails scratched his stomach as my hands made their way up to his chest. His moans spurred me on, I leaned forward to lick around his tiny nipple before I nipped it and moved to the other side. His hands moved from my hips to my ass, once he had a handful, he squeezed, helping me glide up and down.

"Harder, Mercy," he growled. I lost one of his hands for a second before it landed with a sharp smack.

Holy fuck, that felt good. I'd never been spanked, never thought I wanted to be spanked, but the sting of his slap had turned to heat and it shot straight to my pussy.

Jason's mouth was sucking and biting everywhere he could reach, my nipple felt raw, and my neck was sensitive from where he'd nipped. Every part of me tingled with excitement, with an overwhelming energy that threatened to explode.

"God damn, I can't get enough of you. I want to touch you everywhere at once." His hands were moving up and down my back and mine dove into his hair. "I'm gonna come, Mercy."

I was so close, even if he went before me, it wouldn't matter, I'd still be able to get myself off. I rocked harder, grinding down, making sure I put friction on my clit, and tried to catch up.

"So fucking pretty. I don't know what to do with you, Mercy. I can't let you go. Even if it's the right thing, baby. I'm so damn sorry, but I can't." His ass tightened, thrusting up, going deeper, then he froze. "So fucking good."

He groaned his orgasm, closing his eyes with his head tipped back, it looked painful. I wanted to watch the rest of the show but I couldn't focus as pleasure wracked my body, and I shook with the force of the explosion. Jason moved my hips and urged me on. I heard the words but couldn't process what he was saying.

I was spent.

Done.

Emotionally and physically exhausted.

I collapsed on his chest and listened to his heart race as I tried to catch my breath. I'd never had make up sex, or angry sex, or really any sex that involved any sort of high emotional conflict. I had to say, it was good, really good. The next time Jason pulled his Dr. Hotstuff and Mr. Frost routine I knew how I was going to mediate the issue. It was much better than arguing, and highly pleasurable.

"You okay?" He kissed the top of my head and slowed his hands on my back.

"I'm perfect."

"I didn't hurt you?"

Good night, he was too much. Rough and dirty sex god while we were doing the deed and gentle concerned lover when we were done.

"You mean the spanking?"

"Yeah."

"I hope you add that to your repertoire for the future."

"What?"

On a sigh I sat up so he could see me. "Please listen to me. You're not going to hurt me. In case you've missed it, I like rough sex. Or, more to the point, I like when *you* are rough during sex. I like it when you pull my hair. I like hearing you get dirty. I really loved when you spanked me. It shocked the hell out me, but I want you to do it again. I want you to try and do whatever feels natural and good to you. I want the real you, the raw you, not the polite Jason you give the world. I have a feeling you don't show this side of you often."

"I've never shown this side of me to anyone."

"No one?" I eyed him skeptically.

"You sure you wanna know this?"

"Yeah. I wanna know anything you wanna share."

"Right now? While my dick is still inside of you?" His lips twitched into a grin.

Okay, maybe he had a point. I rolled to the side, both of us groaning when I pulled off of his softening dick. I cuddled close to his side, one arm going around his middle, my leg tangling with his.

"All right, I'm ready."

"You sure?"

"I said I was."

Jason took a deep breath and started. "When I started going out with Kayla, I'd only been with one other girl and I was her first. When we were in college, we both agreed we needed to slow our relationship down and take a break. She'd never really dated. I didn't want her to wonder if she'd missed out or was settling. During our time apart, she went out with a few guys, and I was with a few girls. We were not together. She didn't cheat on me, and I didn't cheat on her. Everything was on the up and up and honest. Thinking back, that should've been my first clue.

"Kayla was my best friend, we told each other everything. I knew about the other guys. At the time, I wasn't jealous she'd been with someone else. I thought I was being mature by letting her see what else was out there. Now I know better. Another man touching her should've made me see red, I should've been jealous someone else was kissing her, but I wasn't. So that is the long way of me telling you I've only been with a handful of women. Kayla being the longest. She was sweet, and kind, and soft-spoken. Jesus, I can't believe I'm telling you this." He stopped and fidgeted for a moment before he continued, "And that was the way our lovemaking was. I'm not complaining, or saying I didn't enjoy the time we had together. But it was always gentle, one position. Never in the shower, or against a wall, or bent over a bed. It wasn't rough and raw. I always held a part of myself back because I knew she needed something else from me."

Well, hearing that wasn't pleasant, but neither was it terrible. I could never compete with the ghost of Kayla, nor did I want to. I was me, there was no changing the way I was. I may have been a lot of things, but soft-hearted and gentle were not two of them. I also didn't want Jason to ever hold anything back from me, not even the uncomfortable talks about his sex life before me.

"And with the other girls? Did you ever let yourself go with them?"

"No. For one, I've never trusted anyone enough to allow myself to be real. But I think the biggest thing is, what I feel for you goes beyond wanting to rip your clothes off and get inside of you as quickly as possible. It's more than physically needing you. I want the connection. No, I need it. I can't explain it but when we come together there is this whole other part of me that snaps. I want to consume you, steal your breath, seal you to me, get lost in you. It scares the shit out of me. You quiet all the crazy shit running through my head. You turn me into this wild beast that wants to claim and protect. And, for the record, thinking about another man touching you makes me want to commit murder. When Bruce asked you to lunch, I wanted to kick his ass for even looking at you. I've never been jealous, not once in my entire life have I been possessive."

"I'm glad you trust me." I kissed his chest and sat up. "I want you to know I feel it, too. The connection. The power and soul-deep need when we come together. I don't ever want you to hold out on me. I want all of you, even the scarred and angry parts. Earlier you said you were scared, you'd wanted me to feel your pain and guilt. I want to take those from you, but the only way that happens is if you stop running from what we have."

"I'm not running, Mercy. I'm here, I've told you more than I have anyone else in my life. No one knows we were getting divorced. Once Kayla got sick again, we decided . . ."

"There was no point."

Damn, that was tough. I couldn't imagine going through what he and Kayla had been through. I didn't know what else to say to him, and he didn't look like he wanted to share anymore.

"Thank you for talking to me. For giving me the gift of your trust and honesty. I'll never take it for granted or abuse it." He nodded and closed his eyes. "You staying the night?"

"Yes."

"Flip the light off, would ya?"

He reached over to the nightstand, plunging us into darkness, then he gathered me in his arms and held me tight. Surrounded by the warmth of the bond we were forging, I closed my eyes.

"I'm falling in love with you, Mercy."

"I'll catch you if you promise to catch me."

"I'm fucking terrified."

"So am I."

I knitted our fingers together and settled our joined hands over his heart. The longer I lay there awake, the more I realized. I talked a big game, thought I was tough, and had my life wrapped up so no one could hurt me. But I was wrong. Maybe I'd never truly loved anyone before. Because, as the minutes ticked by, the more I'd come to understand he could destroy me. And, damn, if that wasn't frightening.

WAKING up with a naked Mercy pressed against me was my new favorite way to wake up. I hadn't slept at my house in days. I only went there in the mornings to change for work. Hell, at that point, I never wanted to go back to that house. It felt like a tomb rather than a home anyway. A place where I'd stayed to punish myself for my failures. While inside those four walls I couldn't forget what I'd done. But here in Mercy's house, in her bed, I could breathe. Here, with her wrapped in my arms I wanted to live again. I wanted to let go of the guilt and be the man who would make her happy.

"Morning, baby," she muttered, pressing her ass against my lengthening dick.

That was something else I loved about waking up

next to her; first thing in the morning she was hot for anything I wanted to give her. When she'd woken up yesterday, and before she could roll on top of me, which was her favorite way to wake up, I'd slid between her legs and ate her until she was screaming. And when she returned the favor and sucked me off, I lasted all of two minutes and didn't give the first fuck I couldn't hold back. The second she'd licked around the head of my dick I was ready to come. And when her lips wrapped around my erection and slid down my shaft, swallowing me whole, I was a goner. Her mouth was only second to her pussy. Everything about her turned me on and had me ready to shoot off. It was a miracle I could hold off long enough to make it good for her.

She hadn't been kidding when she'd told me she liked it when I spanked her. I still wasn't sure where the impulse came from, because I sure as shit had never smacked anyone else's ass before, but when her firm bottom came into view all I wanted to do was pinken it. Thank God, she loved it. And by loved it, I mean she went fucking wild when I slapped her ass while taking her from behind. She bucked back, moaned, and came so damn hard I thought she'd snap my dick. Pure perfection. All of it. The sex could not be better.

However, it was more than that. More than simply

wild abandon between the sheets. Anytime I was around her I was happy. Me, Jason Walker, the asshole who'd been living in a self-imposed hell, was happy. And when I wasn't with her, I wanted to be. I wanted to hear her voice, see her pretty face, feel her larger than life presence. She was so honest, it was refreshing. She didn't care if she called me out on my shit. If I started to get quiet, she told me to snap out of it. Everything about Mercy screamed—life.

"Morning, Mercy."

"It's Saturday."

"It is," I confirmed.

"We don't have to get out of bed." Her ass wiggled again. "Have any ideas?"

"Oh, yeah. Spread your legs for me." She was on her side facing away from me, the best she could do was drape her leg over mine, which gave me minimal room, but enough to play. "Wet already," I noted.

"I was dreaming about you."

I pumped my fingers in and out, loving how she rocked with the motion.

"Tell me about it."

I bit down on her shoulder, she moaned, and our telephones started ringing.

"This better be good," I complained, pulling my hand free.

I rolled to the nightstand and grabbed the phone.

"Bruce." I handed her cell to her and rolled again, this time to get out of bed.

I heard her answer her call. I went to the bathroom, shut the door, and answered mine.

"Walker."

"We have fourteen dead kids and three more in the hospital," Scott Mann said.

"Fourteen?"

"Six from Parkside. Eight from Polytech. Three in the ICU are from Parkside. We need you in the office."

"Dammit. Be there in twenty."

I didn't bother going out to get Mercy, I knew she'd just gotten the same intel. I started the shower, stepped in, and waited for her to join me. It didn't take long for her to slip behind me. I offered her a bottle of shampoo, she wordlessly accepted it and started washing her hair.

"All I got was fourteen dead, Bruce give you anything more?"

"No. Just that Keith is coming in and he's bringing in Emma."

"With her parents?"

"No."

"That's going to be a problem. She's a minor."

"Not as of midnight. Today is her eighteenth birthday."

"It's seven a.m. on a Saturday morning. He say why he's with the girl this early?"

"Bruce didn't elaborate. I don't know if he knows. He just said we were needed."

"We or you?"

"He started with *I* was needed and you were his next call. I told him not to bother, you'd already gotten a call, and we'd be in soon."

I wasn't sure why my heart started beating faster. Was it because she'd innocently told Bruce she and I were together this early on a Saturday, and it felt good knowing she had no issue with people knowing we were a thing? Or was it because people would now know we were seeing each other?

"What's wrong?"

Damn, she had an uncanny ability to read my every thought and emotion.

"If Bruce knows, you know the entire department will know by the end of the day."

"Is that a problem for you? I didn't know we were hiding."

Were we hiding? Was I? Was it too soon for everyone to know? Did I want them to know?

With a sigh Mercy yanked back the shower curtain, but before she could step out, I pulled her back in and cradled her to my chest.

"I'm not hiding. And this has nothing to do with

me not wanting people to know how much I love you. This is about me and my shit." Her body had turned to stone, and I wondered what I'd said to make her so upset. "What's wrong?"

"You love me?"

Her pretty eyes looked up at me, and even with wet hair plastered to her head she was the most beautiful thing I'd ever seen. I loved seeing her with no makeup, not that she wore a lot, but with her face wiped clean she looked softer, more vulnerable. Something she didn't show, not to anyone but me. I was the only person who got to know this side of Mercy. And it was only fitting since she got all of me.

"Mercy, baby, I told you I was falling for you."

"Falling is different than fallen."

I didn't mean to chuckle but she was so damn cute I couldn't help it. My laughter died when she balled up her fist and socked my chest. For a little thing she could hit.

"Sorry." With one last chuckle I lowered my mouth to hers and paused. "Yes, I've fallen, so I guess the question is, have you caught me?"

"Yes."

Our lips were still a hairsbreadth apart. "Say it, Mercy. I want the words."

"I love you."

With a primal growl that started in the pit of my

stomach and bubbled its way out of my throat, I closed the distance. Her kiss tasted sweeter—present and future fused, mixed together, and calmness settled over me. A deep-seated love I hadn't known was real filled my soul. I felt every swipe of her tongue, every mew, and the brush of her bare tits in a new and profound way. She'd entrenched herself into my heart.

"If we had more time—" I broke the kiss.

"But we don't. Duty calls."

"Tonight?"

"Mmm . . . tonight we'll—"

"God, please don't say it or we won't be leaving the shower."

"Come on, hot stuff, let's get ready for work."

———

WE DROVE to work in one car, walked in together, put our stuff in her office, walked into a room full of our colleagues, and the world didn't catch on fire. No one said anything, no one batted an eye. My earlier worry seemed ridiculous at best. We were both single, we weren't breaking any rules, and my hang ups, were just that—mine. Kayla had been gone for over two years, and it was no one's business but Mercy's and mine anyway. I was slowly coming back to the land of the living, and it felt good. No, it was great.

"Keith will be here in a few minutes," Scott said. "We have fourteen dead teens, and the media is all over this. Our window is closing."

"The ME's office is putting a rush on the tox screens," Bruce started. "Three juniors, five seniors from Polytech. Three freshmen, a sophomore, and two juniors from Parkside."

"All of the deceased attend the same party? Anything to tie them together?" Ellen, one of the SA's on the case, asked.

"No. Three different parties from what we can tell. We also have three in ICU. Parkside freshmen. Those three were not at a party, but they were all at a park. There was a fourth." Bruce stopped and looked at his notes. "Male, sophomore. He's the one that called it in."

"Who's the ME?" I asked.

"Simon Hines. He was the lead on the Kular case."

"Does he have an opinion, one way or another, whether the fourteen are connected?"

"He believes so, but needs the toxicology reports back before he's willing to swear by it."

"Dammit!" Scott shoved back from the table. "These damn kids don't understand the danger they're putting themselves in. They take whatever shit someone hands them and think they're invincible. And we're always two goddamn steps behind. We shut one person down, and ten more pop up."

Keith and Emma entered the conference room, cutting Scott off from saying anything else.

"I don't have to be here," the girl argued. She looked like hell. Mascara smudged around her eyes, her clothes way too skimpy for a teenager, even one who was now a legal adult. "I told you I want to go home."

"Sit down, Emma," Mercy snapped.

The girl's racoon eyes swung to Mercy, and she narrowed them. Wrong thing to do. "I don't have to be here. He kidnapped me. I said I wanted to go home. I'm gonna call my parents."

"There's not a damn thing your parents can do for you. Now sit down and start talking." Mercy was pissed. "Will someone please get Emma a windbreaker to put on?"

So, I wasn't the only one that noticed her top looked two sizes too small. Keith stood off to the side with his jaw clenched. He looked like he'd had enough of Emma's whining.

"Why don't you start, Keith." Bruce motioned for the undercover narc to start.

Keith walked to the whiteboard and started jotting down names and locations. "So last night started at a girl named Jessica Landon's house." Keith pointed to her name and address. "We showed up at ten p.m.

Emma, here, ditched me fifteen minutes later. While I was wandering around the house wondering where the parents thought their kids were, I heard about a group going to meet with the professor to score. Thirty minutes later, I still couldn't find Emma, I passed a group of kids coming in the door as I left to go search for Emma at one of the other parties." He pointed to the other two addresses he'd written. "I called in the location of the parties and went to the old abandoned drive-in. I find this one here." He stopped again and leveled Emma with a cold hard look. "Around four a.m., hooking up with Pete Sampson, who graduated from Polytech three years ago. Puts him at twenty-one."

"What? Why do you care? I don't see what the big deal is. I broke up with you. You wouldn't even kiss me, you prude. I want to call my parents."

"Yeah, sweetheart, because he's a cop," Mercy informed her.

"You're a cop? How are you a cop, you go to my school?" Emma seemed to be more concerned that Keith was a cop than some of her friends were dead.

"Yeah, she's not the brightest. She'll be lucky to graduate with a D average." Keith shook his head.

"Who's the professor?" Mercy asked Emma.

"How should I know."

Mercy's gaze swung to Keith, he nodded his

encouragement and sat down. The poor kid looked exhausted and I guess he was, he'd been driving around half the night chasing after some high school girl. I remembered Mercy's earlier comment about duct tape and choked back a laugh. I don't know how Keith had kept his cool for as long as he had. Better him than me.

16

ELLEN FINALLY CAME BACK into the room with a blue, extra-large DEA windbreaker and handed it to Emma.

"What's this for?"

Maybe I was fast losing patience because I'd been pulled out of bed bright and early on a Saturday morning. Or because I'd planned on staying in bed all day with Jason. Or maybe because I really didn't want to be at work after our shower where we'd exchanged I love yous. All of those, plus the fact I'd only had one cup of coffee were all very valid points. However, my tolerance for bullshit was at an all time low because fourteen more kids were dead, and three more might die before the day was done, and this little twit was clueless.

"It's for you to wear. You're in a room full of grown

men and your state of undress is making them uncomfortable, and, frankly, it's appalling you'd degrade yourself by wearing so little. So, cover up."

"It's not my fault—"

"Put the damn jacket on. Now!"

I wanted to get her some baby wipes to clean all the makeup off her face, but that would have to wait.

"Am I under arrest?" she asked, pushing her wrist through the arm hole of the overly large jacket.

"Should you be?"

"No. I didn't do anything wrong."

"Start by telling us about the party at Jessica's house."

"What about it? It was boring. She's only a sophomore and she's super uptight." Emma shrugged her shoulders then nodded toward Keith. "He was being an ass, telling me he didn't like how I was dressed. So, when we got to Jess's and Pete texted me he wanted to hook up, I left."

"And what, Pete picked you up and you went straight to the drive-in?"

"No. We drove around."

Christ. Trying to get this girl to talk was like drawing blood from a turnip.

"You do know that some of your friends are dead, right? This is serious. We need to know where you went and what you saw."

Emma's head fell forward, and I thought we were possibly getting somewhere. "I told them after that girl from Parkside got a bad batch it was time to stop. But no one could score anymore benzos or Vicodin so they kept going back."

"Who was dealing the benzos and Vicodin at Polytech?"

"No one really deals it. If someone can get their hands on a script, they sell it. You know someone is always having dental work done, or they pull a muscle at practice. It's not hard. Hell, most of the soccer team fakes hurt knees or ankles and they go to the doctor. Next weekend there's a party." Emma shrugged her shoulders like it was no big deal.

Unbelievable. Complete and total lack of concern. She didn't even bat an eye that her classmates were dead or that what she'd told me was a felony, to her it was nothing. Another day, another party, another night getting high.

"You know how dangerous that is, right?"

"No, it's not. It's not like the other stuff. You get the pills from a real doctor."

I didn't have time to explain to this girl all the reasons why it was, indeed, dangerous.

"You mean the stuff you get from the professor. The GHL."

"The what?"

"The stuff you put in my drink?" Keith told her.

Surprisingly, the stupid girl didn't flinch. "You mean the Gina? I didn't put a lot in there. It's supposed to make you want to have sex—and you wouldn't touch me."

"So, you were going to—" I put my hand up, stopping Keith from finishing.

"Where do we find the professor?" I continued.

"I don't know."

"Who did you get the Gina from?"

Either Emma was dumber than a sack of rocks or she was playing the part. I wasn't sure which.

"A girl from Parkside." I motioned for more information. Emma huffed and continued, "Lizzie. You text her, and she meets you."

"Text her and tell her you want to meet."

"She's only open on Fridays."

Open on Fridays? What the hell, was she a fucking convenience store?

"How you wanna play this, Bruce?" I asked. Still not sure if the girl was telling the truth.

"You don't happen to know Lizzie's last name, do you?" he asked.

"What do I look like, a phone book?" Emma smart assed, crossing her arms over her chest. "I want to go home."

Keith was eying her like he was ready to strangle

her, Jason excused himself from the room, Bruce, Ellen, and Scott ignored her and started talking strategy. I wasn't paying much attention to the plan they were coming up with. I was too busy studying Emma. She would've been a pretty girl if she didn't try so hard. As pissed as I was at her attitude, I couldn't help feeling a little sorry for her. Why did she feel the need to use sex to get attention? What had happened to this teen's self-esteem that she thought sex and drugs were her best options?

She hadn't asked about the kids who'd died, and she didn't ask about the kids in the hospital. Her lack of empathy and compassion annoyed the shit out of me. Was she so self-absorbed she didn't care, or was it all a front? Was she trying to act tough because that was part of her game? Unfortunately, I didn't have time to figure her out, there were kids dying, and if we didn't want more kids to die, we needed to find this professor.

Jason walked back into the room, completely ignoring the pouting teenager, and went straight to Bruce. "I talked to Delaney, she doesn't know anyone named Lizzie, but she still had the after-school science club roster and there is a Lizbeth Cole in the club. They meet every other week after school on a Friday."

"Can you buy GHL every Friday from Lizzie or just twice a month?" Bruce asked.

"Every Friday."

"Still worth looking into," Scott announced.

"This is what's going to happen," Bruce started, pinning Emma in place. "You're gonna go home and keep your mouth shut about everything that went on here today. Monday morning you're going to school and you'll continue to keep your mouth shut. You're also going to stick close to Keith, your wonderful, non-sexual boyfriend. You're going to text this Lizzie girl and tell her you want to make a buy. Tell her you need a lot because a few of your friends want some, too, but you're gonna pick it up for them. Then, Friday, you and Keith are going to meet with Lizzie and pick it up."

"I'm not a rat. I'm not doing it."

"Then you'll be arrested and booked."

"For what? I haven't done anything," she argued.

"Possession of an illicit substance, assault and battery on a police officer, attempted sexual assault, attempted murder—"

"I didn't try to kill anyone!"

"What the hell do you think you were doing when you put GHL in Officer Michaels's drink?" I asked. "You also mixed Viagra with it. You could've killed him. You have no idea what medication he's taking, what his health history is. Wake the fuck up, little girl. You and your friends are playing a dangerous game. And, so we're clear, you will be charged as an adult. You're looking at jail time and lots of it." I'd tried my best to keep my cool, but Emma wasn't getting it. "People are dying. Your friends. And you're sitting here acting like we're inconveniencing you this morning."

"Fine," she huffed. Un-fucking-believable. "But no one is going to believe he's my boyfriend." She pointed to Keith.

"Well, it's your job to convince them."

"Fine. Whatever. Just take me home. I'm tired."

"I bet you are," Keith mumbled under his breath.

"Hang in there, this is almost over," Bruce told him.

"I deserve a goddamn medal for this. You have no idea how . . . challenging this has been."

I couldn't help the laugh that bubbled up. I turned to Jason and lifted a brow. "Think he wishes he had duct tape?"

With a shake of his head and a chuckle he agreed.

Keith waited for Emma to stand, and when she tried to take off the windbreaker to give it back, he told her to keep it on and mumbled something about being uncomfortable being around her when she was dressed the way she was. I didn't blame him, the girl had on less clothes than I wear to the beach. Her boobs nearly popped out of her top and her skirt was extremely short. As they left the room, I couldn't help but wonder if she was one of those kids that took a change of clothes when they left the house. I'd bet she left in an outfit her parents deemed appropriate and changed later. Her clothes were that bad.

After another hour talking about the case and planning for next week, the tox report came in, just as we were leaving. Bruce scanned the reports and confirmed the recipe used to make the GHL was the same that killed Nessa and the fourteen new victims. The local PD was going to have their work cut out for them contending with the media coverage. I just hoped to God whoever this *Professor* was didn't get scared and close up shop before Friday. We needed the buy to go down. One more week and this would be over.

"You ready?" Jason stopped next to me once the meeting was over.

"Yes. I'm starving."

"Me, too." Suddenly, my empty stomach wasn't a priority. Not when Jason was looking at me with his panty-melting, blue eyes. I hated to cook, but if he'd take me home now, I'd make him the biggest damn breakfast he'd ever seen, after we were done giving each other screaming orgasms. "Come on, pretty girl, I know a great little mom and pop place that makes the best pancakes. But if you tell my mom I said that, I'll deny it."

Whoa. Tell his mom?

We said our goodbyes and left together. The walk out was less tense than the walk in had been. When we'd first gotten to the office his head had been on a swivel, checking to see who was watching us. No one cared. I knew there'd be talk after we left, but that was normal office gossip. This morning when I told Bruce he didn't need to call Jason, I'd done it on purpose. Two birds, one stone. I'd let the insinuation hang because if Bruce was indeed asking me on a date, which I thought was unlikely, he'd get the point I wasn't interested without things getting awkward. I also thought it was best to rip the Band-Aid off quickly with Jason. I knew he'd want to hide. I didn't hide. Never have, never will. Even if this was short-lived, I wouldn't be anyone's secret. Thankfully, he'd handled it better than I'd thought he would.

The drive to the diner was quick, and he told me about his conversation with his sister. She was extremely upset about the students who'd overdosed. She also told him she'd poke around, once again he asked her not to, now more than ever, she had to stay clear. The last thing we needed was the case blown because she was snooping around. She'd agreed, but Jason wasn't confident she'd listen.

The hostess seated us, and a very attractive server came to the table straight away, smiling at Jason. I might as well have been invisible. The strange thing was he was oblivious. Her blatant flirting didn't bother me, what did was how unaware he was. It hurt my heart to think about him going through life with blinders on. How much had he really missed?

"Does that happen often?" I asked when the waitress left with our orders.

"What?"

"Seriously? She was totally flirting with you."

"Who? Maggie? No way. She waits on me every time I come in here."

"Right. And why do you think that is? She's totally got the hots for you."

He was quiet for a long time. His gaze was on me, but he'd completely zoned out. It was fascinating to watch as the emotions played across his face until realization dawned.

"I honestly never noticed before. I'm sorry. I've never been interested in her."

"I didn't think you were. You're a good looking man, Jason. I'm sure women hit on you all the time."

"They don't." His face twisted into a grimace. "Or maybe they do, and I've been in my head for so long I never paid attention."

The waitress set our coffee on the table, and Jason fidgeted, not looking up. I said thank you for both of us, and when she left, he mumbled, "Great. Now I feel like an idiot."

With a shake of his head he brought his eyes back to mine and suddenly he looked serious. "I have a question for you. And if your answer is no, I completely understand. I know it's really soon and fast, so if you don't want to, just tell me and—"

"Just ask."

"Tomorrow is Sunday dinner. I know you heard Delaney talk about it, and the other day when I talked to my dad, he mentioned it again. Would you go with me?"

"To dinner at your mom and dad's?"

"Yeah. And my, um, sisters will all be there, too."

"You sure you're ready for that?"

I should've been the one freaking out about meeting his family but I was more worried about him and his state of mind. Delaney had told me Jason had dipped out on most Sunday dinners for the last two years. And over the last year he'd pulled away from everyone in the family. This was a total one-eighty.

"I am. I want you there."

"Why?"

He looked shocked by my question. "What do you mean, why?"

"Why now?"

"Because I'm ready to start living. And now that I've been able to take a full breath of air and really breathe again, I don't want to wait."

"Okay, Jason. I'd love to go."

His hands moved across the table, and he took both of mine in his. "Thank you."

I wasn't sure what he was thanking me for, but it felt nice. Now, if I could keep myself from freaking out, I'd be A-Okay.

17

AFTER A MELLOW MORNING WITH MERCY, I left her house to go to mine. There were a few things I needed to take care of before we headed to dinner tonight at my parents'. Walking into my house felt odd. I was used to the emptiness, I felt *that* every time I entered, but today it was different. No part of the dwelling felt like me, it hadn't taken but an hour for my skin to crawl, and the walls to close in. I didn't belong here, I belonged in Mercy's space. I'd spent the worst of my days in this house, heartbroken, lonely, and slowly falling apart. And that was all before Kayla had died. After Kayla, the guilt over how I'd felt when she was alive had shaken me to my core. If I'd thought I'd felt loneliness and regret while she'd been alive, it was nothing compared to the depth of my despair once she was gone.

All the years we'd spent together, the happy times, the not so happy ones, me failing our relationship, not being able to save her, not talking her into treatment a second time. All of it. Everything swirled together into a perfect storm that tore through my life like a hurricane. Complete with lightning that stopped my heart and thunder that made my ears roar and my mind noisy. I couldn't think in this house. But I'd stayed, ignoring everyone telling me I needed to sell it and move. All because I'd wanted to punish myself. I didn't deserve to find happiness when Kayla couldn't.

I angrily swiped a sweater from a stack in my closet and saw an old shoe box that had belonged to Kayla. Over the first year after Kayla had passed, I'd gone through her things. Some I gave to her parents, some I donated, and some I'd thrown away. I think of all the items I'd gone through, throwing her toothbrush, makeup, and hair stuff away was the hardest. The day I took her shampoo and conditioner out of the shower I'd melted down. Why was I still alive and given a second chance when Kayla wasn't? That may've been the day I'd convinced myself I deserved to suffer, living alone in the house we'd shared. Death had a funny way of fucking with your head.

I grabbed the box and carried it to the bed, opened it, and dumped the contents out. What was left of our lives spilled onto the comforter. Years now fit into one tiny box. The ticket stub from the first movie I'd taken her to, a key ring I'd bought her, the promise necklace I'd given her, and other miscellaneous stuff that, at one time meant something, now mocked me. This was it. An old cell phone and some keepsakes were all I had left. And her wedding rings. Two bands. One I'd slipped on her finger when I asked her to marry me, the other when I promised her a life full of happiness and joy.

For years I'd pondered where I'd gone wrong. At what point had I failed? We were happy in the beginning. We had our whole life planned out, until she got cancer. Six fucking letters that ruined everything. But we'd beaten it together. We'd fought. We'd been strong. A united front as Kayla had battled for her life, and we'd won. We'd grown closer than ever. But any intimacy we'd once had was gone. It was like during that time of extreme trauma we'd become the closest of friends, but the passion and her love for me as her husband had drained away.

The day she told me she thought we should divorce was forever seared into my memory. There was no fight. No argument. It was a conversation between two friends agreeing to dissolve a loveless marriage. Neither of us were upset about it. We still had dinner together that night. We still went to sleep in the same bed. The next morning we had coffee together, even joked that the hardest part about separating was going to be not seeing each other every day. Who does that? What two people who had been married for seven years can just mutually decide to divorce and it be okay? There were no tears on either of our parts. No second-guessing. We both knew it was going to shock our families more than anything because there had never been any outward problems.

The papers were drawn up, and she'd signed them. Then, during a checkup, she'd been told the cancer had returned. She'd still wanted the divorce, but I'd refused to give her one until she got better. I'd been ready to support my best friend again. I knew the toll it had taken the first time around and I wouldn't let her go through it alone. That was when we'd argued. When the tears had streamed down her cheeks. She wanted me to be free. She wanted me to leave her and go find happiness. The argument wasn't pretty. I fought dirty, refusing to give her what she wanted. She relented but made it known she wasn't happy. It didn't matter to me, there was no way I was leaving my friend to go through cancer a second time without me by her side. Thick and thin, that's what we'd promised if nothing else, even if I couldn't love her like a husband should love his wife. She'd been my friend, and I'd stayed.

Standing there in my bedroom I was pondering where I'd gone wrong for a very different reason. I didn't want to repeat the same mistakes with Mercy. Wasn't that a kick in the ass? Trying to puzzle out my relationship with Kayla so I wouldn't lose the woman I loved. I hadn't meant to fall in love. I hadn't meant to fall into her bed, or her arms, or her heart. I'd wanted to live out the rest of my days in misery but, instead, I found Mercy. She'd pulled me in and short circuited my brain. There was nothing I could've done to stop my heart from beating again. My lungs had filled with air, and she'd made me breathe, truly breathe.

If Kayla hadn't died, would she have already found someone to love who'd love her back? Would she be happy for me? Had she really meant what she told me as she died in my arms? Did she want me to move on and be happy? I'd asked myself a thousand times why she'd been taken. Why her? She was so young and full of life. Even if it was in a shy, quiet kind of way. She was so sweet and compassionate. Soft and gentle. Too good to die. Too young to be taken. Even if she was leaving me, she still had time to find true love. *She should've had time.* Fuck! I hated cancer.

Putting everything back in the box, which would sit on a shelf, never providing me with the answers I wanted. But I couldn't bring myself to get rid of it.

I had to get the hell out of this house. Maybe it was time I sold it. I didn't need all this space. Hell, I hadn't needed it when Kayla was alive. We'd known we'd never have kids. Something I hated myself for struggling with. I wanted kids, but, after chemo and radiation, Kayla could no longer conceive. It took me longer than it should've to come to terms with not having children.

I changed my clothes, headed out to my car, and pulled away from the house that was nothing more than a bad memory. I needed to get back to Mercy. I needed to see her. This need deep in my chest had nothing to do with the physical and everything to do with her presence. Just being around her made everything better.

I turned off the ignition, pulled my keys free, and stared at the dangling pieces of metal. Before I'd left, Mercy had slipped her house key on the ring. My heart had pounded then and was now when I thought about the nonchalance of the action. She hadn't made a big deal out of it, simply slid the key on the ring and told me to use it. My mind spun at the meaning. She gave me a key and I was taking her to meet my family. It was too fast, but I couldn't get myself to care. I was living, breathing, and nothing was going to make me slow down. I wanted Mercy and I could no longer find a reason why I shouldn't have her. All of her.

18

"WHENEVER YOU WANT TO LEAVE, we'll go," Jason offered from the driver's seat.

He was nervous enough for both of us. The closer we got, the faster his thumb drummed on the steering wheel. I was trying not to take it personally. It wasn't bringing me home that had him on edge. It was the evening in general. Him bringing someone new home, seeing his parents and his sisters after he'd put so much distance between them. He had to fix it.

In between the most incredible bouts of the best sex I'd ever had, Jason had told me stories about growing up. He was close to his entire family. Or he had been, before Kayla died. I knew Jasper Walker was not his biological dad, but had adopted him when his mom, Emily, married Jasper. There was a story there, and he said he'd share it later. When we talked about his family his face lit up. He missed them. And not just his immediate family, but all of the men he'd grown up with as honorary uncles and their families. There were a lot of them, and I'd had to ask him to repeat some of the names. I'd known that Delaney and Carter Lenox had some distant crazy love affair going on, but I hadn't known Carter had a younger brother, Ethan, who had a daughter. The child was conceived when he was sixteen and still in high school. I was impressed when Jason told me how Ethan had refused to give Carson up for adoption and had raised her alone. He got married not too long ago to a woman named Honor. From the story Jason told, she was perfect for both father and daughter.

He'd also told me about some of the barbeques they'd had over the years. There were eighteen of them who'd grown up together, not including Nick Clark's wife, Meadow, or Honor and Carson. That was a lot of people. A lot of family. I couldn't imagine what it must have been like growing up surrounded by so much love. And they did love each other. Anytime there was a problem, the family rallied as a whole to fix it. Until Jason needed them and he'd pushed them away. On one hand I understood, on the other I was annoyed. I would've given anything to have family around after PJ had died. And especially after my dad had. But I'd had no one. Well, I'd had Tuesday, she'd been there for me.

But no family, no aunts or uncles, no cousins, no siblings to pull together and overcome the tragedy together. Nope. It was me, myself, and I.

"Jason, I'll be fine. Will you be?"

"My parents are going to love you. My sisters are going to talk your ear off."

"Then what are you worried about?"

"I'm afraid to see the hurt in my mom's face."

I'd never asked how close Emily and Kayla had been. I'd assumed close, but I never imagined she'd be hurt by seeing Jason with me. Maybe this wasn't a good idea.

"Because of me?"

"Hell, no. Because of me. I've hurt her. I pulled her family apart."

"Then fix it."

"Easier said than done."

"No, it's not. She loves you. By the stories you've told me they all do. They're hurting because you are. All she wants is for you to reach out and talk to her."

"I can't. She's upset now, but if I told her all the fucked-up shit going through my head, she'd be devastated. That's why I pulled away. I didn't want my misery bleeding into their lives."

He pulled up to the curb in front of a beautiful home and cut the engine.

"It bled into their lives whether you wanted it to or

not. We'll leave when you need to leave. Don't worry about me. I promise I'll be fine."

I hoped that was the truth. I'd never done the meet-the-parents thing. How bad could it be? Have dinner with a group of strangers and hope they liked me. I'd just keep my mouth shut so I didn't blurt out whatever came to mind. Should be a piece of cake. Not. I was a little nervous, a lot more than I was letting on. If Jason's family didn't like me, I had a feeling they'd have no problem telling him, then we'd be done. I didn't want to lose what we'd started.

"Thanks." He tagged me around the back of my neck and pulled me over the center console, meeting me halfway. "I hope you know how much you mean to me. How you just sitting next to me makes everything better, easier. My lungs fill with air and my heart beats. There's something about you that calls to every part of me. I want this, Mercy, what we've started, how I feel when I'm with you. I love going to sleep next to you and waking up with you wrapped around me. I'm in so deep I'm scared shitless. I need to know you're with me. That you want this just as badly as I do."

Oh my gawd, he was killing me. How could he say all of that to me in front of his parents' house seconds before I was going in to meet them for the first time? Now all I was thinking about was going home and throwing myself at him and showing him how much his words meant to me. But that couldn't happen, not yet.

"I'm with you, Jason." His hand flexed on my neck, and I continued, "I want this, too, more than anything I've ever wanted in my whole life. I'm not going anywhere."

His lips touched mine, but instead of deepening the kiss, he placed gentle kisses over my cheek stopping at my ear. "I love you, Mercy James, so damn much."

"I love you, Jason Walker," I whispered back. "Now take me in the house before we have a teenage-style make-out session in your car in front of the house you grew up in."

"That'd be a first. Never made out in my car at my curb before."

"Never?" I scrunched my nose, not believing him. Every teenager had participated in a good old steam-up-the-windows drop-off.

"Never in front of my own house." He chuckled.

I pushed him back and couldn't stop myself from returning his smile. "But you did in front of your dates' houses?"

"No. I was too afraid of getting caught by an angry dad. All goodnight kissing took place down the block from their houses."

"Smart."

"I was a smart kid."

We sat staring at each other for a long time. So long, I was seriously considering ditching dinner and taking him home.

"With those blue eyes of yours, I bet you were a heartbreaker."

"They helped." He smiled.

"I'll bet. All you had to do was bat those pretty long lashes, and the girls were more than eager to jump in a car with you."

"I'm more interested to know if they work on you."

"You know they do."

There was a loud knock on Jason's window, and he closed his eyes before he sighed. "Which one is it?"

"How should I know." I laughed. "It's not Delaney."

Jason looked over his shoulder at one of his sisters, breaking our moment. "Quinn," he announced.

He opened his door, and I followed suit, giving myself a mini pep talk. Everything will be fine. Everything will be fine.

"Mercy, this is Quinn," he introduced us when the two of them met me on the sidewalk.

"Hi, Quinn." Jason walked to my side and grabbed my hand, ready to walk us to the front door. "Nice to meet you."

The girl was staring at us, her mouth opening and closing like a fish gulping for air on land. Great, one sister already speechless, and I hadn't said more than hello.

"Delaney said you were pretty, but, wow, you're gorgeous." She winked at Jason. "Good going, bro."

Jason was stunned. Quinn was smiling like a loon, and I decided I really liked her. She and I were cut from the same filterless cloth.

"You know Hadley and Adalynn were spying from the front window, right?" She laughed. "You're totally busted."

"Clocked them as soon as we pulled up," he informed her.

"What?"

"The twins are nosey. They'd sit by the window and wait for Delaney to get home from a date, so they could tattle and tell Mom and Dad what they saw."

"Oh. Well, we weren't doing anything."

"Right. That's why the windows were damn near fogged up."

"Quinn," Jason admonished. "Don't embarrass Mercy."

Her brows knitted together in concern. "Am I embarrassing you?"

"Hell, no. Takes more than pointing out steamed up windows because I was making out with your brother to embarrass me." I heard a deep, male chuckle that was not Jason's and now I was embarrassed.

"Please tell me that's not your dad and he didn't just hear that."

Quinn's sweet laughter filled the night, and Jason's joined hers.

"I love her," Quinn declared. "Hi, Daddy."

Quinn's eyes went over my shoulder, and I wanted to crawl under a rock and hide. Big fucking mouth already getting me in trouble, and we haven't even made it into the house yet.

"I'm sorry," I whispered.

"Nothing to be sorry for." He kissed the top of my head and turned us around.

Holy smokes. Even in the fading light I could see how good looking Jason's dad was. If he hadn't told me that Jasper was not the man who'd contributed DNA, I'd never have ever known. They looked so similar.

"Dad, this is Mercy James. Mercy, this is my dad, Jasper."

His dad stood a foot from us, eyes glued on our intertwined fingers. I tried to pull our hands apart, but Jason held fast. Finally, after what seemed like an eternity, Jasper's gaze came to mine, and he cleared his throat.

"Pleasure to meet you, Mercy."

"You, too, Mr. Walker."

"Just Jasper. We better get you in the house, my girls are in there itching to meet you."

Oh, boy. The moment of truth was upon us. *Please don't say anything lame.* Jason followed his dad, pulling me behind him. My boots suddenly felt like they were made of cement, with each step they became heavier and heavier.

Of course, Jason would notice. As we stepped over the threshold into his childhood home with his mom and sisters waiting, he leaned down and whispered, "Just breathe."

19

"YOU WORRY TOO MUCH," Hadley said, coming up beside me.

"What?"

"You're watching over her like Mom's gonna say something to offend her."

My sister had it all wrong. I wasn't watching my mom and Mercy because I was worried, I was staring at them because I was amazed at the ease with which Mercy had clicked into place. After the introductions had been made and the small talk had ensued, Mercy had asked if she could help my mom in the kitchen. She sweetly admitted she couldn't cook but was good at cleaning. My mom welcomed her, and Mercy followed her with a single backward glance and a smile.

"I'm not worried, squeak." Hadley smiled at the use of her old nickname.

"Glad you're home, big brother."

Her words hung in the air for a moment before they slammed into my chest. There was no missing the meaning of them. Was I finally home? Could the healing and mending begin? I sure hoped so. I'd missed this, missed seeing my family once a week, missed the connection.

"Sorry I've been such an ass."

"Forgiven." She smiled. "But don't think Adalynn is going to forgive you so quick. You've missed a whole lotta Jake drama."

"Who?"

Hadley's smile faded, and her lips pulled in. *What the hell had I missed? And who the fuck was Jake? I didn't know any Jake.*

"Yeah. That right there is why Lynn's gonna be a little pissed at you."

"Who's Jake? Did he hurt her?" I hadn't meant to growl but the thought of someone putting their hands on my sister and hurting her made me positively murderous.

"God. Now you sound like Dad. Dial it back. Jake was her . . . a boyfriend. He dumped her and broke her heart."

"Where is he now?"

I wanted to find this Jake kid and teach him a lesson about breaking hearts, especially my sister's.

"Afghanistan, I think, or maybe it's Turkey now. She won't talk about it."

"He's in the military?"

"Yeah. The Army."

"Shit."

"That about covers it. Everything was fine until he had to deploy. He broke it off and left."

"What do you mean broke it off?"

"Just dumped her. Told her to lose his number and move on."

"Why didn't she tell me?"

"Huh? Really? You've been a little unavailable lately. And she did call you once to talk about it, and you blew her off."

"Fuck."

I needed some air, needed to think and clear my head. I knew I'd been a dick but I hadn't realized how big of one. I'd turned my back on my baby sister. Being ten years older than the twins should've made it hard to connect to them, but it never was. Often times, they'd come to me for advice before talking to our parents. They'd all crashed at my house on weekends from time to time for some brother-sisters bonding time. I loved when they were around. And I'd turned my back on them. On everyone.

"What's up, Bud?"

I should've known my dad would follow me outside. There was a reason my sisters had come to me, because we couldn't hide anything from Dad. Nothing slipped by him. He always knew what was going on in their lives, but had trusted me to guide them, the same way he had me. And I'd fucked it up. Let him down.

"I fucked everything up."

"Not everything."

That was something else about my dad, he was a straight shooter and didn't mince words. When one of us screwed up, he told us.

"Feels that way. I let you and Mom down. I let Lynn down."

"Yeah, your sister was pretty bummed. That Jake kid fucked her over pretty good. Not that I didn't understand why he did what he did. Kinda like I know why Carter's taken his sweet ass time claiming Delaney."

"Shit." I shouldn't have been surprised, yet there I was with my mouth hanging open.

"What? You don't think all of us haven't seen him dancing around her since she was too young for him to be looking?"

"Well, no. I figured anyone who paid attention would see that."

"Right. So then you understand the only reason I

haven't kicked his ass is because I know he thinks he's doing the right thing by her. Even if, as he's doing it, it's killing her. You know the hardest part of being a parent?"

I shook my head no. I hadn't thought of what it would be like to be a parent. Not in any real way, I'd given up on the possibility of kids a long time ago.

"Watching them hurt and not being able to take the pain. Whether it was Lynn crying over some Army private who'd dumped her because he was leaving on deployment and he wanted her to experience college life. Or Delaney being in love with a man who has a protective streak a mile wide, and Lenox blood coursing through his veins. Which means, he'll martyr himself for the woman he loves more than anything so she won't suffer the possibility of losing him. Or your son pulling into himself because he lost his wife. I have to stand and eat that shit. When all I want to do is take on the pain you're going through so you don't feel a moment of grief. But I can't. You had to go through it, son. You did, and now it's time to start living again."

"I'm trying. But I fucked everything up and I don't know how to fix it."

"You just do."

"Now you sound like Mercy."

"Knew she was smart." My dad leveled me with one of his dad stares and didn't allow me to look away.

"Good thing about family is when you stumble and fuck up, we're here to pick you back up. Lynn's still stumbling. Delaney's still trying to pretend the last visit from Carter didn't affect her. And you're finally back in the land of the living. It's good to have you home, son."

"Mom—"

"Is Mom. Strong, tough, and as gorgeous as ever."

"Seriously?" I chuckled. "That's my mom!"

"I'm aware. She's also my wife. And, son, there hasn't been a day that's gone by that woman hasn't impressed me with the way she loves all of us. She's been waiting for you." A huge smile broke out on my dad's face, and I braced. "It also hasn't escaped my notice she's as beautiful as the day I met her. Maybe it's too soon for me to tell you this, but when you find the woman that means to you, what your mother means to me, there won't be a day you forget it either. Your mom makes me invincible, there's nothing I can't do with her by my side. She's given me five of the greatest kids a man can ask for. One day, son, when you're standing where I'm standing, looking at your children and back on your life, I want your heart to be as full as mine. So goddam full it overflows."

"I want kids," I admitted. "I always have."

I had to close my eyes at the sting. I'd never acknowledged it out loud. Once Kayla couldn't conceive, it was off the table, and no one in my family ever brought it up.

"We know you did. We also know you were setting that part of yourself aside for Kayla." Shit. I hadn't meant to bring Kayla into this conversation. Not when Mercy was here for the first time. "But things have changed. Your circumstances have changed. It's not too late for you to be a dad. I was your age when I met your mom."

We stood in silence. My dad was letting me get my thoughts under control before we went back into the house.

"Thanks," I murmured.

"You never have to thank me for being your dad. I love you, son. And that's why I'm going to recommend we go back in the house now. Your sisters have been with your woman unattended for far too long. You'll be lucky if they haven't already told her the story about them making you pee your pants when you were sixteen."

"I'll strangle them."

"Payback's a bitch, son." My dad clapped me on the back harder than I'd been expecting and I stumbled forward. "Besides, it's pretty damn funny a ten-year-old, an eight-year-old, and two six-year-olds could tackle and tickle their brother until he pissed himself."

"It was a sneak attack. And what was I supposed to

do? The only way to make them stop was to hurt one of them," I grumbled.

"And that's what made you the best big brother those four girls could ever have had. You wouldn't have dared hurt one of them."

My heart ached at his words. "Yet I have."

"Fix it."

We walked into the house, and, sure as shit, my four sisters, my mom, and Mercy were rolling with laughter. I should've been embarrassed since it was at my expense, but, instead, I stood next to my dad and let my heart fill. I knew I was one step closer to what my dad was talking about. One day closer to all the beauty and love he felt when he walked into his house and saw his wife and his kids full of joy.

One day I'd have that.

20

"I'M GONNA STRANGLE MY SISTER," Jason mumbled, walking into my, or should I say our, office.

"Which one?"

It was a toss up which one had annoyed him this morning. Over the last three days since dinner at his parents' he'd called each of them. He'd talked to them one by one, opening up about the last two years and why he'd distanced himself from the family. It took a lot out of him. He'd been emotionally wrecked after each phone call. The last three nights had been intense.

Each night, by the time we'd had dinner, cleaned up, and made it up to bed, he'd been ready to bury himself in me and forget everything. I'd been more than happy to help him forget. Never once had he made me feel used. All his focus and energy had been on me, on what made me feel good. He'd been bossy and rough. It'd been crazy good. Each night he'd let himself go and gave me the gift of him.

"Delaney."

"Oh, boy. What happened?"

"You remember after dinner on Sunday she said she was looking into that science club more because something felt *off*?" I nodded. We'd both told her to leave it alone, we had someone on it, but the woman was Walker-stubborn and said she'd wanted to get the club records to see who was actually going to the after-school meetings. "She said the sign-in sheets were a bust because they're in Mr. Lowe's class and she has no reason to be in there. But she did remember that a teacher, Kimberly Akins, had a thing for the science teacher in the beginning of the year. They went on a date, but, after that, nothing. She also said that Kim has changed. She can't explain how, just that she was quiet and reserved now. Comes in, teaches, and leaves. No more crush on Mr. Lowe, no socializing with the other teachers."

"Shit. That's not good."

"No, it's not. Delaney tried to talk to Kim after a teachers' meeting yesterday after school, but Kim shut her down."

"We need to pass this off to Bruce. See if he can go in and talk to Kimberly Akins."

"She asked if we could do it."

The DEA didn't conduct interviews, not like this. We were merely partnering with the local PD on this more as a sign of goodwill. We should've stepped out of the case when the legal pharmas stopped being used. But Bruce had asked us to stay on and our boss agreed it was good to show the community a group effort, especially because we were dealing with teenagers. They wanted the show of force. However, this was in the local PD's wheelhouse.

"If Bruce doesn't mind, we can head down after school lets out."

"That'd be perfect. I caught a new case," he told me. "Looks like it's coming out of Ohio making its way down south. We're gonna try and intercept it as the shipment goes through Georgia."

Oh. I hadn't given him going back to his task force much thought. I'd gotten used to working with him and sharing an office. Soon he'd have to go back downstairs. That sucked.

"Hey." He stepped around my desk and turned my chair to face him. "You okay?"

"Yeah. Of course. I guess you'll be working out of your office again."

"Soon. But I won't like it." He leaned down placing both his hands on the arm rests of my chair and placed a chaste kiss on my lips. "I've always liked my job, but this last month I've loved it."

"Me, too." Was the only response I could mutter. Him being so close, and smelling his cologne was scrambling my brain.

"The good news is, I get you every night."

"That is good news."

My office phone rang, breaking the spell. "Duty calls, beautiful."

With another simple kiss on my forehead he stood up. Damn work. I wished we were back at my place, wrapped up in each other, in our own world where phones and jobs didn't intrude. But we weren't, and I had to work. Regretfully, I had to answer.

———

THE DAY PASSED by in a flash. Both Jason and I had skipped lunch now that new cases had come down. I'd had to call Bruce and tell him we had roughly a week to wrap this up or he'd only have a skeleton crew from the DEA. Jason was being pulled in a few days, and I only had until next week. The FBI was investigating a nursing home and insurance fraud, they'd passed the case to the DCD because they thought they'd stumbled onto a large number of prescriptions being written and some of those were written to deceased patients. We'd take on the case next week.

It had been a little weird and a whole lot sad not having Jason in my office all afternoon, but we'd both had briefings. He'd only come up when it was time to go to Parkside to try and catch Kimberly before she left for the day.

"Can I ask you something?" I turned in the passenger seat to face Jason.

"Sure."

I took a moment to appreciate how good looking he was. There was something about a man driving that was sexy. With his dress shirt sleeves rolled up, I could see the muscles in his forearms bunching while he gripped the steering wheel. I wondered if that's what they looked like when he hooked my leg in the crook of his arm and held me in place while he was on top of me. Suddenly I wondered if I'd be able to see them if I had a mirrored ceiling. Or would I be too busy watching his backside as his ass flexed as he pushed into me? Oh, God, that would be so hot. His back and shoulders were well defined, I bet those would be—

"Mercy?" He chuckled. "You got something you want to share?"

"No."

"By the pretty blush on your cheeks, I think you do."

"No. No. Nothing to share."

"All right then. What did you want to ask?"

Oh, yeah, I had a question.

"Why are we always in my space?"

"What?" His forehead furrowed and his hands flexed on the wheel.

"You moved up to my office when you could've asked me to come down to yours. There's more room in yours. We always end up at my house. And you've never invited me to yours."

"Is that a problem for you?"

My first thought was no, it wasn't, but the more I thought about it, it became more complicated than a simple no.

"I guess it depends on why."

We were almost to the school, and he was still quiet, which worried me. I thought we'd moved past the silence and secrets. I was formulating my next question when he pulled into the school's parking lot and answered.

"I never gave much thought about why I went up into your office. Honestly, I started working in there because I wanted to be close to you, get to know you. I wanted your attention but I wasn't in a place where I knew how to ask for it. My house . . ." He parked and exhaled. "Is not a happy place. I can't breathe when I'm there. When I'm at your house I'm at peace. I'm surrounded by you. Your place feels like home, mine feels like a jail cell."

"It doesn't have anything to do with it being the house you shared with Kayla?"

"It has everything to do with that." Shit. That kinda stung. "It's the house I shared with her. The place where my marriage failed. Where she and I had battled her cancer, where we worked out our separation, where I was happy, where I was unhappy, where she died. Why would I want to invite you to a house where there isn't a place that doesn't hold some fucked up memory."

"But all your memories in that house aren't bad. There were happy times there."

"There were. While the memories were being made, I was happy. I lived with my best friend, we laughed and had fun. We goofed off, my sisters came over, we were happy."

"Then I don't get it. Other than the obvious. Why do you think all the memories are now bad?"

"Did you hear what I said? I lived with her as my friend. Not as my wife. I failed—"

"Bullshit. You failed nothing. You didn't fail her, nor did she fail you. Sometimes things don't work out. But you gave her the greatest gift in the world—your friendship. Do you know how lucky the both of you were to have that? There are so many people that never have a true and deep friendship like the two of you shared. Some people's marriages end but they were never close friends in the first place, and things get horribly ugly. That's not what happened with the two of you. Your friendship weathered the storm. You need to stop beating yourself up for things that were not your fault. I'm not speaking ill of Kayla, but she had a part in your marriage not working out, too. She was the other half of the equation that you want to sweep under the rug. I get it. I really do. But, Jason, enough. You've tortured yourself long enough."

"I'm trying."

"Shit. I know you are. I didn't mean to—"

"Don't apologize. One of the many things I love about you is you don't pull punches. Please don't start now. I need you to know, I'm letting go of the past. I'm moving forward. But there are things that are going to take longer than others to get over. Sunday when I was at the house, I was thinking it's time to sell it."

"Wow. You were?"

"My parents wanted me to move out immediately. But I couldn't. And not for the reasons they thought. I wasn't holding onto a ghost. I wanted to be punished and living in Kayla's home was like a life sentence of guilt and self-reprimand. I don't want to live like that— not anymore."

"Good."

"Got any more questions?" His grin told me he was trying to be a smartass not a jerk.

"No."

"Let's go talk to Kimberly. When we're done, I'll drop you back at the office and hit the grocery store on the way home. Neither of us had lunch, and I'm starving."

Home.

"Are you saying you're cooking tonight?"

"Sweetheart, there are a million reasons why I love you. Cooking is not one of them."

I tried to hold back my smile but failed. "Okay."

I was still stuck on his home comment. Him acknowledging the fact I was a horrible cook didn't faze me one bit.

21

WE'D INTERVIEWED Kimberly Akins as gingerly as we could. Delaney was right, something had happened on the date she had with Derek Lowe, but she wasn't talking. We couldn't press because we were there under the pretense of talking to her about the students who'd overdosed. Kimberly had been open and very emotional when we talked to her about the students, but when we steered the conversation to the science club and the students who'd been involved in the after-school activity, she shut down and gave short answers.

When we left, Mercy had called Bruce and told him he definitely needed to be looking into Lowe. Even the moniker, the professor, fit with the dealer being a teacher. After Mercy finished with Bruce, I called Delaney and told her she was to stay away from Lowe. Completely. No more asking around. No more looking into the club. One hundred percent out of it. I pressed, she agreed.

It was after dinner and Mercy and I were curled up on her couch when she said, "Tell me something about your childhood."

I thought back to all the family get-togethers, all the crazy shit my cousins and I used to get into, but there was one thing that stuck out. One event that had changed my life and had forever cemented my relationship with my dad.

"I was kidnapped when I was six."

"What?" She sat up and stared at me with her mouth hanging open.

"So, you know that Jasper adopted me." She nodded. "My mom was in an abusive relationship with a man who was also into criminal activity when she got pregnant with me. Her friend, Steven, found her beaten and at rock bottom. He packed her up and took her back to Georgia with him. During the drive she told Steven she was pregnant. He drove straight to the courthouse and married her the same day."

"Wow. Where's Steven now?"

"He was in the Army and was killed in action when I was a kid. I was kidnapped by a man named Liam Gains. He was the man my mom had run from."

"Your real—"

"There's nothing real about that coward. Jasper's

my real dad. And before Jasper, Steven was the man who saved my mom and claimed me as his son. Liam was never anything other than a woman beater and drug dealer."

"You're right. I'm sorry."

I hadn't meant to snap at Mercy, but even after all these years thinking about Liam putting his hands on my mom and hitting her made my blood boil. There were many factors that came into play when I decided to join the DEA; my mom's brother, Brian, was one, and stopping men like Liam was another. Growing up I'd always known I wanted to be like my dad, I wanted to protect and serve. I just didn't know how I wanted to do that. I'd assumed I'd join the Army like my dad and uncles but when my cousin, Nick, went into the FBI, I realized there were other ways I could serve my country here at home.

"Sorry, I didn't mean to cut you off." I pulled her back into my arms and kissed the top of her head, stopping to inhale the soothing scent of her hair. It always smelled fresh and like flowers. "Anyway. When my mom left Liam, she took something of his. When I was six, he decided he wanted it back and took me in exchange. I was only with Liam a couple of hours, Jasper tracked him down to an abandoned hunting shack and came and got me."

But in those few hours I had been scared out of my

six-year-old mind. It wasn't that Liam had physically hurt me, though I did see him hurt my mom when he took me from the car. When Liam dragged me away, I saw my mom bleeding and begging him not to take me. I wanted my mom. I wanted Jasper.

"Where's Liam now?"

"Dead."

Jasper had smashed through the door of the cabin, and, even at six, I knew he was not the same loving man that had made my mom smile, or the same man who'd played with me. He was an avenging warrior. He looked bigger that day— meaner. Jasper had told me to close my eyes, but I'd peeked. Watching Jasper slit Liam's throat should've made me more scared, but it didn't. That was the moment I realized there was nothing Jasper wouldn't do for me. He saved me. He came for me. And he killed the man who'd taken me.

"Did . . ."

"Yes, he did."

"Good."

We both sat in silence, and I remembered what my dad had told me on the phone the other day, there was nothing I'd gone through that my parents hadn't already experienced. I'd thought about the parallels, and he was right. Jasper had lost his best friend, and the child she'd been carrying. He knew loss. He'd almost lost my mom, too, when he couldn't get over the guilt.

Steven had scooped up my mom and married her, simply because she'd been his friend, not because he loved her. They'd lived together as husband and wife, but it had been a lie, they were only friends. Both of my parents knew what I'd gone through, in their own way, yet I'd pushed them away.

"Hey." Mercy's soft voice pulled me back to the present. "Where'd you go?"

"Sorry. Just thinking."

"I gathered that. Wanna share?"

"Nothing to share really. I'm just happy to be sitting here with you. I hope you know there's no place I'd rather be. I want to tell you everything, all my secrets. I want you to go back to my parents' house with me for Sunday dinners. I want you to meet the rest of my family at the next get-together. I want to invite my family to our house for a barbeque. I want you to feel like they're your family as much as they're mine."

"I'd like that, too."

"Tell me about PJ."

"You know how people always say so-and-so was a good person who just made bad choices?"

"Yeah, sure."

"Well, I don't think that was my brother. When we

were kids, he was okay, nice to me, normal. But the older he got the less he seemed to care about those around him. Actually, he didn't care much about anything. By the time he was in high school he was a self-absorbed ass. He was the one other parents warned their kids to stay away from. Something was just broken in him. My dad tried to help him, but PJ never saw a problem with his "I don't give a fuck" attitude. Drugs were kind of a natural progression, I guess. I knew he smoked pot, did pills, but I didn't know he'd gotten into the rave scene. The months leading up to his death were bad. My dad was at a loss, he tried to get him into rehab, but PJ would do his thirty days, get out, and then go right back to his previous behavior. I wonder if it was chemical dependency or if he was addicted to self-destruction. Tuesday was there, she saw it, too. She tried to help PJ even though he was older than us, but he shut her down and refused to let anyone in."

"Damn, sweetheart. That's rough."

"It was. I never wanted my brother to die. And I was really angry at him for a long time, at my dad, too. But after my dad died, I realized that holding on to all the anger wasn't doing me any good. Bad shit happens all the time. They were gone, but I wasn't. Yet I was still allowing my brother's behavior to affect my life. My dad's need for revenge cost him his life, but it was his life to give. I had to let go and move on. There wasn't any other viable option. I was alone in the world and if I didn't do it, no one was going to do it for me."

Mercy's strength and determination impressed me, but it also served as a reminder she was so much stronger than me. I'd wallowed in self-pity for so long, I'd stopped living. I'd gone through the daily routine of getting up and going to work but I was empty. Hollow. Numb. I'd thought that was the way my life was meant to be but, now, I realized I'd been a cowardly prick.

"How's Tuesday?" I asked, trying to move the conversation to something less heavy.

"She's good. Having fun in Germany. She sent me an email yesterday. She'll be back next week."

"Fashion show, right?"

I remembered Mercy telling me Tuesday was going to Italy then Germany for work. I thought she said fashion show but it could've been for a photoshoot.

"Yep. I hope you're ready to meet her."

Why did something so simple as Mercy wanting me to meet her friend make my heart beat faster? My vibrating phone cut off all good thoughts when I read the text that had come through.

DELANEY: I have a problem. Fucked up. Call me.

Now my heart was pounding for a new reason. My

sister was in trouble. I immediately dialed her number and she picked up on the first ring.

"Hey, Dad."

Dad?

"Where are you?"

"Oh, no. Is she all right? Which hospital?"

"What the fuck's going on?"

"Okay. I'm having dinner with a friend but I'll leave now. See you in ten minutes."

Delaney hung up and Mercy was staring at me.

"What was that about?" she asked.

"I have no idea. Either she's in trouble or on a bad date and needed an excuse to leave."

"Does she date?"

"Fuck no."

I stood from the couch and began pacing. I'd give her five minutes to call me back then I was calling my dad for reinforcements. Mercy watched, not saying a word, but the worry on her face matched mine. What the hell had Delaney gotten herself into?

Her time was almost up when she called me back.

"Where are you?"

"In my car. I screwed up. I'm so sorry."

"Are you safe?"

"Yeah."

Now that I knew my sister was safe, I couldn't hold back my agitation. "What the fuck happened?"

"Can I come over?"

"I'm at Mercy's . . ." I rattled off the address, and when my sister told me she'd be over in ten minutes, we hung up.

"Well?"

"Shit, Mercy, I didn't even think to ask if she could come by."

With a wave of her hand she said, "She's welcome anytime. Is she okay?"

I was a damn lucky man to have a woman as good as Mercy in my life. She didn't care I was bringing family drama into her home, she'd welcome my sister and whatever issues came with her. Her only concern was if she was okay.

God, please don't let me screw this up.

22

AFTER DELANEY HAD MADE it over, all hell broke loose. Brother and sister had gone to war. Jason was pissed, not that I blamed him. He'd repeatedly asked Delaney to stay away from Derek Lowe. Yet she'd wound up sitting across from him at dinner after he'd caught her following him. Now we were fucked.

Apparently, Delaney had been minding her own business at the grocery store when she saw Derek. He'd been on his phone, and she'd overheard him saying there'd be enough for Friday and he was going to go pick it up. Instead of calling Jason and telling him what she'd heard, she'd decided to follow him. Not knowing he was going to a storage facility that was at the end of a dead-end road. Once she'd been behind him at the gate to enter the fenced-in building, she was stuck. When Derek had looked in his rearview mirror and saw her, she panicked and followed him through the gate. At least she was smart enough to come up with a story on the fly and told him she had a unit there, too. Then she'd had to make an excuse that she'd left the right key at home. Stuck in a bad situation when he asked her to dinner, she'd agreed.

Texting Jason and having him call with a made-up emergency had been the smartest thing she'd done. Jason had gone bananas. He'd been furious with her, and it hadn't mattered how many times she said she was sorry, it had done no good. I'd felt bad for Delaney, but she'd put herself in serious danger. We still didn't know what happened to Kimberly Akins, but at this point, if I had to guess, I'd say Derek had slipped her something and then taken advantage of her. How far Derek had gone, was up for speculation since Kimberly wouldn't talk. But Delaney sitting across from the man that was smack dab in the center of a drug ring investigation didn't sit well. Not for me, and especially not for Jason.

We'd called Bruce, and he was going to work on getting a search warrant, though it was going to be difficult. All we had was a hearsay conversation that could have meant anything. But the detective was going to do his best and try to push it through. It was well after two a.m. before we'd crawled into bed, with Delaney safely tucked away in my guest bedroom. I think she'd agreed without argument because she was freaked out.

This morning, Bruce had phoned and told us he'd called in every favor owed to him to get a warrant for the storage unit and Derek's house. Delaney had also agreed to call in sick to work and stay at my house while the warrants were being served. The plan was to hit the house at five a.m. before Derek left for school. The storage unit would be hit at the same time by a second team.

We'd geared up and were following Bruce and his guys to Derek's home address. The plan was simple. Surround the house and knock on the front door. He had no registered guns in his name, though we knew that didn't mean shit. Just because we'd thought the search would be easy it didn't mean we weren't prepared for the worst. Jason had been stoic and silent most of the morning. One-word answers and even those were given miserly. Grunts seemed to be what he preferred in his current mood.

"Two minutes out," Bruce crackled in my earpiece.

"Copy that," I called back.

"You know she thought—"

"Don't make excuses for her. We both asked, and she promised to stay away from him."

"I know. But—"

"No buts. She got lucky. There's no telling what he

could've done to her. What if she'd taken a drink from her soda? What if she couldn't have left, and he'd taken her home?"

We didn't know if Derek had tried to slip Delaney anything. Jason was just going down the rabbit hole of what-ifs.

"What if, she gave us the break we needed, and we stop a new batch of GHL from hitting the streets? What if, because of Delaney, lives are saved? I know why you're mad, I am, too. But, and don't interrupt me, she was smart and got herself out of the shit she'd put herself in. She's at home, safe and sound. Don't spend the rest of the day playing out worst case scenarios in your head. No good will come from it. She feels bad. She knows she was wrong. She's been properly chastised. You kicking the dead horse and beating her up some more just makes you a dick, Jason. Let it go."

He mumbled something I'm sure would've pissed me off, so I didn't ask him to repeat it. We were both dog-ass tired and getting ready to go into a high-risk situation. We both needed clear heads and to be on our game.

We met the breach team on the lawn and jogged to the door. After two pounding knocks, Bruce waited a moment before he told his man to break in the door. Bruce peeled off left, and, with my weapon drawn I went right with Jason behind me. We cleared the living room and the kitchen, finding both empty.

"Upstairs," Jason said, taking the lead.

Two of the local guys followed us up, breaking away once we hit the upstairs landing.

"Got something." Came through my earpiece.

Jason and I continued into the master bedroom. "Is that the shower?" he asked.

"Sounds like it."

"Shit." I let Jason breach the bathroom door not wanting to have to pull a naked Derek out of the shower.

"DEA, put your hands where I can see them!" Jason yelled.

"What the fuck?" Derek returned.

"Turn the water off and step out of the shower."

"Can I grab a towel?"

There was silence for a moment before Jason's back came into view, his gun still out in front of him. Both men appeared in the bedroom and, instead of the embarrassment I thought I'd find on Derek's face at being forcibly removed from the shower at gunpoint, when his eyes landed on me a sly smirk crossed his face.

"Well, hello."

"Shut the fuck up and put some pants on."

And that was my cue to turn around. Normally I

wouldn't have cared, I'd seen my fair share of perps in all manners of undress, but I didn't like the look on Derek's face.

"You don't need to turn. I'm not shy."

"Clothes," Jason growled.

"We have lab equipment," Bruce said through the comm.

"Put your hands behind your back," Jason told Derek.

Once Derek was cuffed, I holstered my weapon and watched Jason take him by the arm and walk him down the stairs. I went into the room next to the master bedroom and was shocked at the sophisticated lab Derek had. Metal shelves lined the walls with rows of chemicals neatly arranged. A full shelf of over the counter cough syrup and stacked boxes of sinus medication was below that. On the floor there were gallon jugs of different solvents. All of that was bad, but the scales, glass beakers, Bunsen burners, and vials rounded out his setup.

"He's making more than GHL," I noted.

"I'd say you're right."

Derek Lowe had a full-on meth lab next to his bedroom, in a nice house, in a nice neighborhood. And, to add insult to injury, he was a teacher. A man the community had trusted to teach and guide their children.

"Good, clean takedown today, James. Appreciate all the help from your team," Bruce said. "Ready to take this asshole downtown and see if he's ready to talk?"

"Absolutely."

I made my way downstairs, hoping Jason would be in a better mood now that Lowe was in custody. And the sole reason behind the easy bust was Delaney. The sun was barely over the horizon and we had a drug dealer off the streets. All in all it was a great day.

23

EVEN THOUGH DEREK LOWE was technically the local drug task force's bust there was still an outrageous amount of paperwork that had to be filled out. Lowe's interrogation had been short. The second he was behind the table in the interview room he'd lawyered up. As a matter of fact, he'd said nothing after I'd cuffed him. Not a single word had slipped past his foul lips. He wouldn't even confirm his name was Derek Lowe until he sat at the table and said lawyer.

I'd given a lot of thought to what Mercy had said about how tough I'd been on Delaney. She was right, I had been hard on my sister but the thought of what Lowe could've done to her made me go ballistic. And after his smug ass was arrested it hadn't made it any better. The guy was a complete scumbag. His home lab was a testament to how dangerous he really was. But because Delaney had followed Derek, we hit pay dirt. We were able to take him at home without incident. At the end of the day, no one had been hurt and Lowe was off the streets.

I owed Delaney a small apology and a huge thank you. I pulled into Mercy's driveway happy to see Delaney's car still parked in the driveway. She and Mercy must still be talking. After we'd left the office Mercy was going straight home, and I'd gone to pick up my dry cleaning.

When I'd walked in the door I hadn't expected to find my mom sitting on the couch next to Mercy and Delaney. The three of them all had wine glasses in their hands and they were laughing. What the hell was going on?

"Hey," I greeted them.

Mercy smiled, Delaney looked shy, and my mom was beaming.

"Hi, son."

"Did I miss your car outside?"

"No. Dad dropped me off. He'll be back in a few minutes, he went to pick up a pizza."

Well, damn. I hoped someone had thought to ask Mercy and they hadn't just invited themselves over. My family had a tiny problem with boundaries, as in, they didn't have any. When my parents had wanted to see me, they just showed up. If they wanted to have dinner they came over with food in hand and invited themselves in. Same with my sisters. A pang in my stomach hit me hard, they hadn't just shown up in a long time. They'd called and asked, and when I'd said I wasn't up for company they'd mumble their disappointment and leave me to my brooding. Shit. I was an asshole.

"I invited them," Mercy spoke up. "I didn't think you'd mind."

Mind?

It was her house. I was a live-in guest in her home. I wasn't sure how I was supposed to respond to her statement, and the longer I stood there the stupider I felt.

"Come here, Mercy."

She got up from the couch and when she was within reaching distance, I tugged her into my arms and buried my face in her neck. "Thank you," I whispered.

I felt her nod, and she held me tighter. I wasn't sure what I was thankful for exactly but I was appreciative of something. I was lost in my own world surrounded by Mercy's scent and her warmth as we embraced. I thought I heard someone sniffle but, before I could look, there was a knock on the front door, and I heard my dad.

"Yo. I'm back."

I closed my eyes against the emotions threatening

to bubble up. How many times have I heard my dad enter a room with a, "yo"? And how long had it been since I've heard it? Too damn long.

"Good, you're home," he started. "What's your take on this Lowe asshole?"

He walked past us not giving us, locked in an embrace, a second glance and set the pizza boxes down on the kitchen table.

"I'd say he's pretty much screwed. The reports coming in show traces of methamphetamines and GHL in his lab. His storage unit came up with liquid GHL already dosed out and ready for distribution. He also had gram bags of his homemade meth ready to sell. When I left, the narc we had in place at Polytech had brought in two high school girls for questioning."

"Fucking scumbag," my dad said under his breath. "Who's hungry?"

"You ready?" Mercy quietly asked.

"Are you sure about this?"

"Positive." I kept my eyes trained on hers for any signs she wasn't telling the truth. "I bought this house a few years ago. I've lived in it alone. No family. The only person who'd ever been here for dinner was Tuesday. So, yes, I'm ready. This is the first time since I've lived here it's felt like a home."

"Damn, I love you."

I didn't have to look away this time to confirm I'd

heard sniffling. And I knew it'd come from my mom. When Mercy broke away with a chaste kiss and walked to the kitchen, my family didn't bother trying to hide. They'd heard. They'd watched our interaction. They also didn't try to cover their smiles. And in my mom's case, tears. Damn, I'd been such an ass.

The hours passed in a blink. We ate, the women drank wine, Dad and I had a few beers, but mostly we laughed. It was the best night I'd had in as long as I could remember. When my parents were getting ready to leave, they both pulled Mercy in for a hug. My mom held onto her for a long time, I couldn't hear what she said but I knew she was telling Mercy something in a hushed voice.

Delaney moved closer to me and murmured that Mom had been losing it all night and tearing up. I pulled my sister in for a hug. "Sorry, sis. I may've over-reacted."

"You didn't. I get it, I screwed up. After Dad gave me a dressing down he reminded me of all the ways I could've screwed up your investigation. I didn't mean—"

"I know you didn't. You also didn't have all the facts. The mere thought of someone hurting you makes me see red."

"I love you, big bro." Then she leaned in closer and

whispered, "All teasing aside about Mom, I'm really happy for you. You deserve this."

"I'm not—"

"Well, I am. I'm positive, and little sisters are always right."

"I missed you, sis."

"Ditto. I'm gonna drag Mom out of here for you. You can add it to the list of favors you owe me."

Damn, I'd missed this closeness with my family. Missed the dinners and laughter. True to her word, Delaney pulled Mom out the door, leaving me alone with Mercy. She'd never looked more beautiful than in that moment. Big smile on her face, relaxed and happy. What was even better than her pretty grin was that she was looking at me like she was hungry.

"Thank you for tonight," I told her.

"It was fun."

"It was."

She stepped closer to me, her eyes raking over my body as she moved. "You tired?"

"Not even a little bit."

"Good." Mercy stopped in front of me and gathered the hem of my T-shirt in her hands and started to lift. "I need you."

"Here?" I looked around the living room, already knowing where I was going to take her.

Mercy didn't answer, instead she pulled my shirt

up and over my head. She quickly followed, yanking hers off and tossing it next to mine. Her eyes didn't waver, they remained glued to mine as her pants, then panties, fell away.

"You're still dressed," she noted.

"I am."

I tugged her closer, her perfect, perky tits against my bare chest. My mouth went to her neck, her head tilted to the side, and she moaned. I knew every sweet spot, every place that would make her grind into me and writhe. I played with both of her pink tipped tits, sucking and nipping her nipples into tiny, hard nubs. I alternated between near-painful bites and gentle swipes of my tongue. Both I knew drove her wild. And, tonight, I wanted wild.

"Are you wet for me?" I asked as my hand was making its way south.

I knew the answer before she could mutter her confirmation. I toyed with her wet folds, not giving her what she wanted. Not yet. I wanted her begging first.

"Bend over the couch." Mercy did as I said. "More. Rest your cheek on the cushion. I want your ass in the air." She lowered herself more, and my hands roamed. Down the silky skin of her back to her firm ass. "You have a great ass."

With a swat that was just enough to pull a groan from her sweet lips, I went back to teasing her. Circling her opening until she pushed back trying to impale herself on my fingers. I pulled my hand away and went back to her ass, kneading and massaging the pink mark I'd left.

"Please."

"Please what, Mercy?" Her ass wiggled, and she pushed back. "That's not an answer."

"I want you inside of me."

"Like this?" I roughly thrusted two fingers inside her heat and didn't let up. "Is this what you want?"

"Oh, God. Yes."

I continued to finger her until her hips bucked and her inner walls started tightening. I pulled my fingers free and went back to teasing her slit.

"Jason!"

"Hmm?"

"I'm so close. Please."

"What do you want?" I asked.

"I want you to fuck me."

There were the words I wanted to hear. I made quick work of releasing my dick from the confines of my slacks and pressed the head to her drenched pussy. In a single thrust I was fully enveloped in her heat.

"Yes."

I curled over her back, biting her shoulder before I kissed away the sting. "Is this what you need?"

"Yes."

My mouth worked her neck, up to her ear, and back down again as I pounded into her from behind. Home. Bliss. Love. Warmth. The feel of her wrapped around my dick pulled every emotion from me and merged them with the physical pleasure only her body could provide. I was mindless in my pursuit of ecstasy. Tingling heat started at the base of my spine, euphoria started to take over. I needed her to go with me.

"Reach down and play with your clit."

I unfolded and grabbed her hip with one hand and used the other to rub her backside. I didn't have to see to know her fingers had found the sensitive bundle of nerves. Mercy's erratic movements told me she was rubbing herself.

"I'm close," she moaned. "So fucking close, Jason."

I couldn't stop the sensations from barreling forward if I'd tried. It was too good. *She* was too good. Fluttering in her pussy started, and it would only be seconds before she exploded, and the clench of her orgasm would detonate mine.

With two consecutive hard smacks to her ass and with a growl I demanded, "Come for me. Now, Mercy. Right fucking now."

I planted as deep as I could and let go. I didn't need to move, Mercy bucking and her inner muscles tightening was all it took. My head fell forward, and my release shot out of my dick with such force I couldn't keep my eyes open.

"Mercy!"

Never had I ever loved someone so thoroughly and completely. Physically, mentally, with an all-consuming soul need.

24

A WEEK HAD SLID by in the blink of an eye.

I don't think I'd ever been happier it was a Friday. Jason's new case had kept him busy throughout the work week, some days he hadn't been in the office at all. A major deal was going down. A motorcycle club from Ohio wanted to move product through another MC's territory. We had a local informant inside the club, and he'd tipped off Jason's task force. Negotiations were underway and the shipment was due to pass through our stretch of I-95 at anytime.

The FBI had punted a pharma lead to my division. After a week digging through prescriptions written to dead patients of the nursing home, we knew we were onto something big.

Jason had texted me he was already home and was

cooking. Tuesday was home and finally coming over to meet Jason. I don't know why I was nervous. They'd spoken on the phone several times, Tuesday was like-able, Jason was sweet and funny; I knew they'd hit it off. But I couldn't shake this dread in the pit of my stomach.

Everything was going great. We were totally compatible in every way. I was even thinking about asking him if he wanted to move in. Which may've been a little fast, but I've always done what I wanted, when I wanted. I lived by my own set of rules, and neither of us cared what other people thought of our relationship. But what had started as a tingle this morning after Jason had left for work before me had turned into a nag by the end of the day.

Nothing had changed, Jason was Jason, loving, kind, and considerate. He'd brought me a cup of coffee into the bathroom as I got ready for work. He'd smiled, kissed me, told me he loved me, and was out the door. But there was still this feeling. I didn't like it. I didn't want anything to ruin our night with Tuesday. I'd missed my best friend and couldn't wait to hear all about her travels.

I made my way into the house and found Jason in the kitchen.

"There you are." He smiled.

He pulled me in for a kiss, which I happily returned, muttering how much he'd missed me.

"You just saw me before you left." I pecked his cheek and looked around. "Wow. It smells wonderful in here."

"I thought I'd make something easy. It's Honor's recipe."

"She's married to Ethan, right?"

"Good memory."

"I feel like I should take notes when you tell me about your family. Maybe once I put faces with the names it will be easier to remember them all." Jason stared at me with a funny look and I tried to backtrack. "I mean, that is, if you want me to meet them. One day, I mean. When you're—"

"Sh." He placed a finger on my lips. "I love that you want to meet the rest of my family."

He lowered his head and took my mouth in a panty-melting kiss that made me wish Tuesday wasn't coming until later.

As if on cue I heard her raspy voice call out from the front door, "Hey. I'm here."

Jason broke the kiss, and I muttered, "Remind me to take away her key."

"Wow. Sorry. I didn't mean to interrupt," Tuesday said.

I broke away from Jason and all but skipped to my friend, pulling her into a bear hug. "I missed you."

"No, you didn't." She laughed.

"I did so."

"Um. No. You didn't. How could you with all of that to keep you occupied?"

Tuesday's hand motioned to Jason, his face blushing under my friend's compliment. I couldn't stop the laugh that broke free at seeing Jason embarrassed.

"You got me there. He is pretty cute."

Jason shifted from side to side, clearly uncomfortable. Which only made me want to continue.

"Cute? Honey, I work with male models all day long. And they got nothing on him." Tuesday pointed at Jason, and his face blossomed from pink to cherry-red.

"Yeah. He's a keeper for sure." Deciding to have pity on Jason with him not knowing Tuesday and her flair for dramatics I thought it was better to cut him a break. "Jason, this is Tuesday Knowls, international model extraordinaire. Tuesday, this is Jason."

"What? I don't get anything after my name?" Jason joked.

"Oh, I could throw in some adjectives but I thought I'd save those for girl talk later."

With a groan and a shake of his head he offered

Tuesday his hand, followed by a nice to meet you. Tuesday looked at his hand and laughed. Stepping up to him she wrapped her arms around him and squeezed.

"Hand shakes are for strangers. Hugs are for the man that has made my friend ridiculously happy."

I heard Jason chuckle and as the shock of Tuesday's attack wore off, he hugged her back.

After they broke apart Tuesday looked around the kitchen and her mouth dropped open. "And you cook? I know that delicious smell from whatever is on the stove is not coming from something Mercy made."

"Hey. That's . . ." I couldn't think of anything to say other than to point out the obvious.

"The truth," Tuesday finished my sentence. "It is no secret you can't cook, friend."

"I know. But, jeez, you don't have to remind him."

"Baby, I've told you a hundred times, there are many, many reasons why I love you. You not knowing how to cook doesn't even register."

"I think I just swooned. Please tell me you have a brother."

"Sorry. Four sisters."

"Do they all look like you?"

"Yep. They are all stunning," I answered for Jason.

"Damn. Your poor dad."

Jason chuckled and shook his head. "Dad? What

about me? I've had to threaten every teenager within fifty miles to stay away from them."

"Ah. The overprotective type. Nice."

"Damn right."

Jason went to the kitchen to finish dinner, and Tuesday eyed his ass as he walked away.

"Tuesday," I snapped.

"What? I just wanted to make sure he looked just as good from the backside."

Jason barked a laugh and I shook my head. "If you're done ogling my man's ass, I'll get you something to drink."

"I wasn't ogling. I only ogle available men's butts. I was merely making sure—"

"Right."

I knew Tuesday wouldn't touch Jason with a ten-foot pole. She was just being her normal, crazy self. Nothing she said or did shocked me anymore. If there was one thing Tuesday was, it was loyal. She'd never betray our friendship.

Dinner went just how I knew it would. Tuesday and Jason hit it off. We all sat around and laughed until we cried. Tuesday told us wild stories about her time in Italy and Germany. Everything from wardrobe malfunctions to prima donna, diva models walking off of the set of photoshoots. She had us in stitches with all her tales.

By the time Tuesday left I was exhausted. I didn't protest when Jason walked us upstairs, stripped me naked, put me in bed, and tucked me close to his chest. I was asleep within minutes. I should've felt great after the night we'd had. But my heart was heavy.

25

AS MUCH AS I'd love to stay in bed with Mercy all day, I had a surprise. She didn't know we had plans for the day, but we did. And if she didn't stop grinding her ass on me, we wouldn't be getting out of this bed, and we'd be late.

"Morning," she yawned.

"Sleep well?"

"Mmm."

"I'll take that as a yes."

I started to roll away when she caught my arm. "What's the hurry? It's Saturday."

"Come on. We have plans."

"Plans?" she groaned. "And they involve us not being in bed all day?"

"Yep. I'm taking you somewhere."

"Where?"

"It's a surprise." Mercy turned and buried her head in her pillow. I knifed up, pulling the covers back as I went. Now it was my turn to groan. Creamy naked flesh greeted my eyes. "Up you go. Before I change my mind."

She rolled to her back, cupping her breasts as she went. "You sure we can't stay here?"

"You're killing me."

"Oh, all right. I'll get up. Do I have time to shower first?"

My mouth had gone dry at the sight of her. "Yep. I'll start the coffee."

I grabbed the pants I'd kicked off last night and shoved my feet through them and fled the room. She was too tempting. We'd spent a lot of time together. Mostly locked away in her house. I wanted to take her out on a date, do something fun.

I waited in the kitchen for the coffee to finish brewing and loaded the dishwasher and cleaned up the last of the dinner mess. The shower turned off, signaling it was now safe for me to return to the bedroom.

Yes, I was that weak. I needed to wait until she was done and dried off before I reentered. Two cups of coffee in hand I made my way back into the room. I set my coffee down on the nightstand and was happy to see Mercy was dressed and had a towel around her wet hair when I entered the bathroom.

She turned, and my eyes narrowed. What the fuck? Was that a hypodermic needle between her teeth? She had her shorts pulled down on one side, exposing her hip. I watched as she cleaned the area with an alcohol square before she took the needle from her mouth and gave herself an injection.

"What the fuck?"

"Oh, sorry, are you squeamish around needles?" She recapped the syringe and used the alcohol swab to rub the injection site.

Was I squeamish around needles? Had she lost her fucking mind? No. I was goddamn pissed my girlfriend was injecting herself with something.

In an instant white-hot fear took over my body. Memories flooded. All the times I'd had to give Kayla a needle when she was going through cancer treatment. Cleaning her ports, changing her bandages.

"Are you okay?"

Mercy's voice barely registered through my haze.

"Are you sick?" I finally spat out.

"I have pernicious anemia," she answered.

"What?"

"My body lacks a protein. Intrinsic factor. It doesn't absorb B12 and it causes me to have a low red blood cell count."

I couldn't pull my eyes from the needle now on the vanity top. It was like a red, flashing warning light. Mercy was sick. Low red blood cells. I knew all about low blood counts. White. Red. Platelets. Blood transfusions. Bone marrow. Chemo. Radiation. Been there.

"Jason?"

My gaze traveled from the offending needle to her pretty face. She didn't look sick. But neither had Kayla—before. Why would Mercy do this to me? Why would the universe? Two women. Both sick. This was my punishment. My reminder I didn't deserve to be happy. I was a failure.

"I can't do this."

"What?" Confusion marred her features.

I couldn't speak. I couldn't formulate a coherent sentence, not with the fucking needle mocking me. I started to back out of the bathroom. I needed to leave.

"Don't do this, Jason. I'm not sick. Just stop for a minute and let me explain."

Explain?

"I can't, Mercy. I'm sorry. I need to leave."

"Please." I didn't need to face her to hear the tears.

I grabbed the rest of my clothes off the floor and quickly dressed. I was dizzy, and the coffee I'd barely sipped was threatening to make a reappearance.

Fuck.

"Don't walk out on me, Jason."

"I'm sorry."

"If you're sorry then stay and listen to me. You need to breathe."

I didn't need to breathe, I needed to leave. I was going to hyperventilate at any moment. I couldn't stop the onslaught of emotions, the biggest one was fear. Dread wasn't far behind. I was almost at the front door when Mercy's sob tore through my heart.

"You said you loved me." My hand froze on the doorknob. "If you walk out that door all you're proving is you never loved me. You never meant anything you've said to me. And once you prove yourself to be a liar, the bridge will be burned. I'm begging you one more time to stay and talk to me about this. All I need is five minutes, and you'll understand."

"I love you, Mercy. But I can't stay. I can't do this again. I'm sorry."

I opened the door and cursed the crisp fall air as it hit me in the face. I couldn't remember the drive back to my house but the next thing I knew I was walking in my front door.

I couldn't breathe.

I never wanted to breathe again.

"Fuck!" I roared and slammed the door. Shutting out the world. Closing off my life to love—to Mercy.

26

I'D SPENT two days in bed.

Two days sobbing.

Two days trying to purge every feeling I had for Jason out of my system. It hadn't worked. Funny how before Jason had come along, I'd never felt lonely. I could always find some way to entertain myself, occupy my time, be happy. But now that I knew a man like Jason existed, I was lonely. My bed felt too big. My house too empty.

I'd ignored Tuesday's many calls. I didn't want to talk, have to explain that Jason had left me over my monthly B12 injection. Why hadn't I talked to him about it sooner? *Because it wasn't a big deal, that's why.* There was nothing wrong with me that a simple vitamin shot couldn't fix. I wasn't dying. I wasn't sick. If I missed a shot my symptoms were fatigue and headaches. I didn't even take medication, it was a vitamin for God's sake.

He'd left me.

I'd begged him not to, and he'd walked out the door.

I'd never dreaded going to work before, but, today, I wanted to be anywhere but there. I was sure I looked like a haggard mess, even after I'd spent an hour trying to cover the dark circles under my eyes. All I wanted to do was stay holed up in my office and not leave. Thank God, the case we'd been working on was wrapped up and I didn't have to work with him. That would have killed me.

I'd come in thirty minutes early this morning so I could rush upstairs and not run into him. I needed to snap out of this shit. This wasn't me. I didn't avoid—I hit shit straight on.

My landline rang, and I jumped. *Get it together, Mercy.*

"James."

"There you are. Finally come up for a breather?" Tuesday. I groaned not wanting to have this conversation at work. "What's wrong?"

"Nothing . . . everything. Can I call you when I get home?"

"Not with an answer like that you can't. What are you doing for lunch?"

"Working."

"Bullshit. You're meeting me at the deli."

I knew what deli she was talking about. It was our go-to eatery when we met on my lunch hour.

"Seriously. No time today. I have a—"

"Make time."

"Tuesday—"

"We're having lunch, final answer. If you're not there at noon I'll go by your office and ask Jason where you are."

"Don't do that," I seethed.

"Thought so."

What in the world was she talking about? I was too tired to talk around a riddle. Lunch with Tuesday was not what I needed. She'd want to rehash every detail of my very painful last conversation with Jason.

"I'm not sure what you think you know. But I really can't do lunch. Please."

"Damn. Fine. But I'll be over tonight with a bottle of wine and Chinese. If you're not there. I'll wait all night if I have to."

"Chinese won't help this time," I breathed.

"Didn't think it would, sweets. Neither will the wine. But you and me, we can get through anything."

I had to fight back the tears when Tuesday's whispered words hit my broken heart. She'd been my *person* for so long I didn't know what I'd do without her. Normally she had all the answers. She was my sounding board. But I wasn't sure she could help sooth this particular ache in my chest. No one could.

"Thanks."

"Always. See you tonight."

I replaced the receiver and sat back in my chair. I didn't want to discuss Jason—at all. But at least Tuesday caved and would wait until after work.

Time seemed to creep by, I must've checked the clock every ten minutes. Even the hour-long conversation with the FBI agent in charge of the fraud case against the nursing home hadn't taken my mind off my problems. After my dad had died, work had been my salvation. I'd been able to throw myself into my caseload and forget I was without siblings and an orphan. I had no one to pick me up and dust me off. No mother to cry to and get advice from. A father to be outraged on my behalf and promise to protect me from the evils of the world. I thought I'd found something special in Jason. I stupidly thought he was *the one*. On second thought he *was* the one—the one who would finally break me. The one whom I'd taken my armor off for, and he'd trampled the gift I'd given him.

I left five minutes earlier than normal and quickened my pace when I hit the bottom floor. My heart pounded in my chest as I scurried past Jason's office. I tried my best not to look in the direction of his door but

I still caught the room in my peripheral. The lights were off, he wasn't even in, and there I was trying to escape the building without him seeing me.

By the time I made it to my car, my breathing was almost back to normal. God, I was so weak. I couldn't recall the drive home if my life depended on it. One minute I was in the DEA parking lot, the next I was pulling into my garage. I numbly walked into my house and was greeted with nothingness. No aroma of dinner being made. The smell of Jason's cologne was noticeably absent. Just nothing. An empty house, with a bunch of memories I wanted to forget but couldn't.

I hated that my heart was shattered, that I could remember every touch, every sweet word, every cuddle on the couch, my bed, the shower. Damn them all. Damn him. Why did he make me fall in love with him only to turn and push me out of his life? And what was so wrong with me that I desperately wanted to hear his voice? See his smile one more time instead of the anguish that marred his handsome face. Screw that. So what if he was good looking. There were a lot of handsome men out there. And who cared if he knew exactly what I needed before I did, that was just sex, really good, awesome sex. Sex and love are two different things. He never loved me anyway. I was on the right track. The more I told myself lies the more pissed I became. Anger was my friend. Rage would get me through this heartbreak. It had to.

The front door swung open, and I despised myself for hoping. For holding my breath.

"Hey," Tuesday said.

My lips drew in, and I pinched them together as hard as I could as disappointment raced through my body. Damn, I was stupid. He wasn't coming back. Not today. Not ever.

"Oh, shit," she muttered and jogged to me, pulling me into a hug. "Shit, Mercy."

The unwanted tears streamed down my face. I didn't bother to wipe them away. Now that the faucet had opened there was no stopping them.

"He's gone," I admitted.

She didn't reply. There was nothing to say. Standing in the middle of the living room I thanked my lucky stars for my friend. The only tried and true person in my life. And then I promised myself I'd never feel this pain again.

27

IT HAD BEEN the worst week of my life and that was saying something. All the feelings I thought I'd worked through about Kayla had come rushing back with a vengeance. Ugly shit I never wanted to think about again looped in my mind. Kayla dying in my arms morphed into Mercy holding onto me, begging me not to leave her. My dreams confused the two, and I was tortured nightly by Mercy dying.

I hated myself for hurting her. I was a failure and a fucking coward—two times over.

The banging on my front door pulled me from my self-recrimination. No one other than my family would pound on my front door on a Saturday morning. They'd all repeatedly called me, and I'd sent them all to voicemail. I couldn't tell them what I'd done. How badly I'd screwed up again. The only question was who was here? My dad, my mom, my sisters? I didn't want to face any of them.

"Glad to see you're breathing." My dad stepped into the kitchen where I was pouring myself coffee.

I didn't bother answering. He wasn't looking for one anyway. By the look on his face, he was pissed. Yet another fuck-up on my part.

"How long has it been since you've talked to Mercy?"

"A week."

"Thought so." My dad studied me with a look that could only be described as disappointment. At least I hoped it was and not disgust. Though, I couldn't blame him if it was. I was pretty disgusted with myself. "So you're back to living in this hell hole with the curtains closed, moping, pacing the floor, and feeling sorry for yourself?"

"What the fuck? Sorry for myself? My wife died, and that's what you call it?"

"How long do you think you're gonna play that card?"

What in the actual hell? Who was this man? The dad I knew was strong and compassionate. He'd had high expectations of us, punished us when necessary, but he'd always handled us with care. This was the cool Special Operator he kept away from the family. If he'd wanted the kill shot, he'd succeeded.

"Until I'm over it."

"You'll never be over it. Wanna know why?" He didn't give me a chance to answer. "Because you won't let yourself be. You hide behind it. You wallow in your misplaced guilt. I've watched my son, for goddamn years slowly waste away. No more, Jason. Not one more fucking day will I watch. Get over yourself."

I wasn't sure what hurt more. My dad's revulsion or that he'd called me Jason. He'd called me Bud since the day he met me when I was six. Never Jason.

"Guilt—"

"Do not try and bullshit me. I am intimately familiar with the feeling. I lived and breathed regret and guilt for years. I can smell its stench anywhere. And you reek of it. It oozes from your pores. You did everything you could for Kayla. There is nothing for you to feel guilty about."

"I didn't do anything for her but fail her."

"No, you—"

"You have no idea what you're talking about!" I shouted.

"You did everything you could," he repeated.

"Except love her." My dad froze. I bet he hadn't seen that coming. I bet he would've never guessed that the boy he'd raised to be a man was a fraud. "She deserved a man that loved her the way a husband should. A man that desperately wanted to make love to her. Adored her. Want to touch and cuddle her close. That was not us. That man was not me. She knew it. I knew it. Everything was a fucking lie, Dad. Everything. She was finally leaving me. She was supposed to finally get everything she deserved. Then she got sick again, and I refused to give her the divorce she wanted. So you tell me how I did everything I could for her. Huh? Now you know what a fuck-up I really am. My wife was leaving me."

"I know, Bud."

"What?"

I could barely catch my breath; the room was starting to spin. Surely, I'd heard him wrong. He couldn't have known. We played the part of husband and wife in public perfectly. Our friendship wasn't an act, it was easy to fool everyone around us.

"Kayla talked to me and your mom before she filed."

"She did what?" They'd known all along? Pretended like they didn't. What the fuck? "And you never told me?"

"She wanted to make sure we understood why the two of you were separating. She didn't want us to be mad at her. Honestly, it didn't come as a surprise."

Glad my parents weren't shocked by my impending divorce. What else had they been holding back about?

"Well, it surprised the fuck out of me."

"No, it didn't. If you look back over your marriage you knew. It's just easier to lie to yourself and pretend the obvious wasn't in front of your face."

"What's next? You're gonna tell me you never liked Kayla?"

"We loved her like a daughter. But we knew she was not the woman you'd spend the rest of your life with."

"What?"

"Kayla was your first love. It was young and it was a learning kind of love. She taught you how to be a man. And you showed her how a man should treat her. You two were fast friends, you shared a deep bond, one that was shrouded in friendship, not soul-binding, intoxicating forever love. You were her caretaker, the person she turned to for advice, you were her biggest cheerleader. She gave back to you as much as you gave her. But anyone with eyes in their heads could see that neither of you looked at the other with all consuming adoration. There was no spark. Friendship, yes. Lust and love, no." My dad stopped and sucked in a breath.

"We all miss her. She was sweet and kind. A genuine good person. She caught the worst deal life could throw at her. But you gave her everything you could until her last breath on this earth. She knew how much she meant to you. She understood you were willing to stay in a relationship with her for the rest of your life if that's what she wanted. You were content in your arrangement. But, son, you didn't have a marriage."

What the hell was I supposed to say to that? He was mostly right. I was content in our arrangement. I was roommates with one of the best people I knew. She was funny and sweet. We had a good time together even if there was no intimacy. Once sex was off the table, it was like a weight had lifted, and, once again, we could go back to being friends like we'd been before we walked down the aisle. At one time, I'd thought there was a spark in our marriage. Wasn't there? Hadn't I felt lust-drunk in her presence? *Not the way I'd been when I was with Mercy.* Hadn't I felt an all-consuming need for Kayla? I hung my head in shame, I'd never felt passion and want as deeply as I'd felt with Mercy.

"I can't see her anymore when I close my eyes," I admitted.

"You're not supposed to. You have to let her go. It's time. You hold your good memories close. You remember the good friend she was to you and let the rest go. You can't keep doing this to yourself."

"I ran out on Mercy," I told him.

"I gathered that. Why?"

"I walked in on her giving herself a shot."

"A shot? What kind of shot?"

"A B12 injection. She has pernicious anemia."

"You left her because she's anemic?" my dad asked in disbelief.

I could feel the panic bubbling up, bile crawling up my throat. I didn't know what was worse, seeing Mercy and the needle or her face when I left.

"I saw the syringe and lost it. I felt like all the air was being squeezed from my lungs. My worst nightmare had come to life right in front of my eyes. I couldn't hear what she was saying over the roaring in my ears. I had to leave, get away from all the memories and images. All I could see was Mercy dying in my arms. Losing my best friend nearly killed me. If I lost Mercy I wouldn't survive. The fucking needle was sitting on the counter, something so stupid and innocent turned into a venomous snake waiting to strike. I couldn't think, Dad. All I could do was run. I walked out on her as she was begging me to stay and talk."

Damn, I was a heartless bastard. So fucking dumb. I'd left the woman I loved over a needle. Weak.

"You can still make this right. You have to talk to her."

"It's too late. She told me if I left, we were over."

"Nothing is ever too late. Did you know I left your mom?"

"What? No. When?"

My dad's face clouded over as he remembered a time I was sure was painful. How did I not know this either?

"You know how I know what you're going through? Because I've been there. I didn't only lose a friend, I lost the mother of my child *and* my daughter. I was broken. I couldn't get over what I'd done. Then I met your mom and I thought I had, until she mentioned having more kids. I spiraled and left her. Next thing I knew I was on a plane headed to my hometown. I had so much guilt and self-hatred I didn't know what to do with it. I went straight to Liz's sister's house and prayed she'd tell me what an asshole I was and I didn't deserve to be forgiven. But not your Aunt Reagan. She told me to get over myself, move on, that it was what Liz would've wanted. I ran home to your mom and begged her forgiveness. The difference between a woman and a man is a woman will fall in love with the idea of you, the future, the promise they see in you. They will wait, give you more chances than you deserve. Your mom gave me the chance I needed to prove I was the man she thought I was. But you need to pull your head out of your ass and go to her, now. Time is not your friend. The longer this lingers the harder it will be to fix it. And the promise I see in Mercy, the beauty she gives you, the future you could have are worth fighting for— do not delay. You don't want to wake up a year from now, alone in your bed, with nothing but regret to keep you warm. Trust me. You will have lost a good woman. One who supported you while you were struggling. Even if that support was remaining quiet so you could figure your shit out. She was still by your side."

My dad was right. I would regret losing Mercy. Hell, I regretted it now. I missed her so fucking much I couldn't see straight. There was a hole in my heart that only she could fill. It was hers. Every part of me was.

"I don't know how to fix it."

"You start by opening your damn curtains. Letting some sunshine into this pit of gloom. You open your eyes and see the people around you who have your back. You beg, plead, and fall to your knees. Crawl if you have to. You exhaust every recourse, then you find more. What you do not do is give up. I didn't raise a quitter, don't start now. You need to be the man I know you are. Honest. Kind. Goodhearted. Be the man she needs you to be."

I could beg. I would beg. I'd crawl back to her if it meant this ache in my heart would subside.

28

I'D LIKE to say I was feeling better after talking to Tuesday, but that would be a lie. It would also be a lie if I said that through my hectic work week, I hadn't had time to think about Jason. As busy as the last few days have been, I still found the time. I still missed him and loved him just as much as I did when I woke up the morning he'd left me ten days ago. Ten horrible fucking days.

He hadn't been into the office the last three days. I'd heard the task force was out in the field. The rival MCs had come to an agreement and they were moving product down I-95. The shipment was supposed to be intercepted sometime today. They'd used the first two days for surveillance. It was a big shipment, and the MC had sent extra security to ensure the eighteen-wheeler packed full of drugs made it to the drop.

My cell phone vibrated with an incoming text and I thought about ignoring it. I knew Tuesday meant well, but I didn't need her checking on me every five minutes. The phone vibrated again and I knew she wouldn't stop.

DELANEY WALKER: I think I'm in trouble.

DELANEY WALKER: No thinking. I'm fucked. Derek Lowe is following me.

Fuck.

I pressed the call button and waited. Three rings then to voicemail. I sent her a text hoping she'd answer.

ME: Where are you?

I jumped up, grabbed my keys, and flew down the stairs. I jumped the last two, jogged to the heavy glass doors, and pushed. Cool air blasted me in the face as I took off in a sprint to get to my car.

ME: Delaney! Where are you? I'm on my way.

It was just after eight a.m. She had to be in class. I pulled out of the lot, trying to call Delaney while driving sixty in a twenty-five, with cars lining both sides of the two-lane side street. Goddamn it. Why hadn't I looked at my phone sooner?

Again, no answer.

I dialed Bruce, he could get someone to run a trace on Delaney's cell.

"Detective—"

"Bruce, it's Mercy. Listen, I need you to track

Delaney Liberty Walker's cell phone. She texted me that she was in trouble. Derek Lowe is following her. How is that possible?"

"Damn it. Where are you?"

"Headed to Parkside. Delaney should be in class."

"I'll get someone on the trace and meet you there. Is Jason with you?"

My heart constricted but I didn't have time to think about my broken heart, Delaney was in trouble.

"No, he's in the field. Even if I tried, they're radio silent."

"He's gonna flip his shit. See you in fifteen." He wasn't wrong; Jason was going to have a heart attack. I was breaking every traffic law known to man getting to the high school. I hoped fifteen minutes wasn't fifteen minutes too late.

I pressed Delaney's number again, and this time it went straight to voicemail. That wasn't a good sign. Either her phone was dead or turned off. If that was the case, we were fucked. There was no way to trace her cell if it wasn't pinging towers.

Dread bloomed. The last time I'd felt this feeling in my gut, Jason had left me. I pulled into the parking lot and scanned the area. Delaney's car was not in the teachers' lot. That could mean any number of things. I pulled in front of the building, parked in front of the red curb, busses only section, and jumped out, not bothering to turn my car off.

I buzzed the door, banged on the glass, and waved my credentials in front of the camera.

"May I help you?"

"Agent James, DEA. I need to speak with Delaney Walker immediately."

The door clicked, allowing me to enter. A woman met me in the lobby before I could turn toward Delaney's classroom.

"Agent James. Ms. Walker isn't here today. Is there an issue? Something I can help you with?"

"What do you mean not here? When did she leave?"

"She had a scheduled day off. I believe she was going to the dentist or doctor. May I help you?"

"No. Thanks."

Think, Mercy. Shit. Jasper.

I scrolled through my contacts pulling up a number I never thought I'd need, but happy Jason insisted I program it in—*just in case.*

"Hello?"

"Jasper? It's Mercy."

"What's wrong? Where are you?"

What the hell was it with Walker men, did they have a special Spidey sense?

"I'm at Parkside looking for Delaney. I got a text

from her saying she was in trouble, Derek Lowe was following her. I have local PD trying to triangulate but her phone is now off. She's not at school. Something about an appointment. Do you know where she was going this morning? I need a place to start searching."

"Derek Lowe?" The deadly tone sent shivers down my spine.

"Jasper! Where was her appointment?"

"Didn't know she had one. Let me call Em."

He hung up, and I was stuck with my thumb up my ass with no starting point. Bruce should be pulling in any minute. We could split up and search for her.

My cell phone buzzed with an incoming text.

DELANEY WALKER: Promises. Promises. You can't be on your way because you don't know where she is.

Oh, God. Lowe has her. I needed to engage him. The longer the phone was back on the better.

ME: Derek. You don't want to do this. Delaney has nothing to do with anything. I'm the one you want.

DELANEY WALKER: You want her? Come get her. You have five minutes.

ME: Where?

DELANEY WALKER: Corner of Fifth and Channel. Behind the old waffle place. Five minutes and we roll.

I sped out of the lot and called Jasper.

"No luck."

"Lowe contacted me. The old waffle house on Fifth—"

"I know it."

"He said if I'm not there in five he rolls and takes her with him. I'm four minutes out."

"You got back up? I'm at least twenty out."

"Negative. I don't have time to wait."

"Stand down, Mercy. Don't go in alone. We'll track him."

"Not a chance. She doesn't spend one more minute alone with him than she has to."

"Mercy—"

"Hanging up now, Jasper. See ya when you get there."

I was coming up on the corner. I needed a plan. There was no way I was letting Delaney go anywhere with Derek Lowe.

My phone rang and I sent it to voicemail. I didn't have time to argue with Jasper. I pulled into the alleyway and Derek was standing next to Delaney's car, gun pointed to her temple. I hit the redial button, heard Jasper yelling, and I told him the only thing I could that would possibly save us.

"Her car."

I clicked off the call, silenced my phone, pulled my gun from my holster, and got out.

"You don't want to do this, Lowe. Let her go." I sounded like a parrot.

"Right. Drop your weapon and get in."

"No. Let her go, and I'll go with you."

"Look at you, thinking you're in control. You've got until three and we end this right here."

"You shoot her, I kill you."

"I've got nothing to lose. I don't give the first fuck. You two bitches cost me everything. Three. Two—"

"Okay." I slowly lowered my weapon. I dropped the magazine out and tossed the gun under my car.

"Get in the back seat." All three of us started to approach the car. "What do you think you're gonna do with that?" Lowe motioned to the polymer magazine in my hand.

"I'm not leaving a loaded gun on the ground." I shoved the seventeen-round mag in my back pocket and climbed in.

Delaney was roughly shoved through the driver's side door and told to crawl into the passenger seat. I wanted to tell her to jump out and run, but Lowe was in the car, reversing before I could.

"Where are we going?" I asked.

"To have one last party."

My blood ran cold. I didn't think he meant the fun kind of party with balloons and clowns.

"By the way, give Delaney your phone."

He pointed his pistol at her, and when I handed it to her, he told her to toss it out the window.

Well, there went that plan. Our only hope now was Jasper. I prayed he understood my last two words to him or they truly may have been my last.

29

"TF ONE, YOU READ ME?"

"Loud and clear," I told command.

Comm check complete, we were almost ready to intercept. Twenty-five DEA agents, twenty bikers, and a shipment of narcotics worth high six-figures. What could go wrong?

It had started with fifteen bikers following the semi-truck, those numbers I could stomach. Twenty-five to fifteen and the odds were in our favor. But this morning five more had shown up as the eighteen-wheeler pulled out of the truck stop. I didn't like our current state of play. We were only five up on a bunch of one-percenters, a biker gang that lived and died by a code of brotherhood. They wouldn't go down easy. There would be no surrender with them.

We all knew we had a battle on our hands, and,

just like all the operations before, our only hope was we'd have the tactical advantage and our training would prove superior. Bullets don't discriminate. All it takes is one lucky shot and you were dead.

Let's hope luck would be on our side today.

Team one was to cut the bikers off from the rig. Team two would take the shipment.

"We're ready to move. Do *not* trust any of these fuckers. They'd sooner gut you than wind up in lock-up," my team leader barked in my ear.

"Copy that. TF One in place and ready."

"Move out."

Monroe and Evan pulled out with four agents in each of their heavily armored suburbans. They'd go ahead and get in front of the rig. Sampson pulled out with his four-man team, and I followed with three other men in my truck. We'd catch up to the Harleys and pull in front of them, cutting off their access to the semi. Lawrence and Tito would come in behind the bikers and box them in.

The two lead vehicles were in place and Sampson and I took our places in front of the bikes, slowing down and swerving so they couldn't pass us on the two-lane access road. It was important we took out the caravan before they hit I-95. There would be too many innocent civilians in danger if a shootout took place there.

"TF One. Slow your speed."

"Copy," Sampson answered.

I let off the gas and followed his lead. We were down to ten miles an hour.

"Anyone think it's odd no one's tried to pass us?" I asked.

"Just thinking the same thing," Tito answered.

"We're ready to roll the rig to a stop on your go, TF One," Monroe came over the radio.

"We're down to five miles per hour. Start your deceleration," I answered.

Something was definitely wrong. The bikers should be showing some signs of distress but they were simply rolling to a stop. No one tried to break away, no guns were drawn.

"This is jacked. This is too damn easy."

Sampson and I rolled to a stop and waited for twenty-five bikes to follow suit. Let the showdown begin. Doors opened, and DEA agents descended, barking orders for everyone to keep their hands on their bars. Every biker complied. Front and center was a bearded man, late forties, with tattoos covering both arms and his neck. The front patch on his cut read President.

The man didn't move as I approached, weapon drawn and on high alert. "How ya doing this afternoon, agent?" He looked like he didn't have a care in the world.

"Just out for a leisurely ride?" I asked. "You don't have any weapons or contraband on you, do you?"

"Nope. Just a pocket knife."

"Mind if you ask your boys to dismount and consent to a search?"

"Sure." His hand shot up in the air and with a finger pointed to the sky he circled his hand. "Spread 'em, boys, you're getting a DEA special today. Maybe even a happy ending if one feels so inclined."

"Rig's empty. I repeat, rig is empty. Not even a pallet," Evan barked in my ear. "Goddammit."

I patted down Mr. Smart-Ass President and he was telling the truth. A legal pocket knife was the only thing he had on him.

"So what is this?" I asked, gesturing to the gang of men behind him.

His eyes flared and brow pulled down. "Just taking care of some club business."

"Business, huh? You're a long way from home to be taking care of business. And coming into another MC's territory to do it? Seems like bullshit to me."

"Sometimes you have to eat up miles to find a man's loyalty."

Well, fuck. This was a dry run. They'd thought they had a mole, and now it was confirmed. I didn't know who our source was and, even if I did, there was nothing I could do. Even locking the man up wouldn't save his life. You live by their code, you died by it.

"We're clear. No one has shit on them," Lawrence announced. "Command, waiting for your orders."

The agent back at headquarters let a string of curses fly before he said, "Cut 'em loose."

"You all have a safe trip home," I told the biker.

"Aces, let's ride."

DEA agents all stepped to the side as the Harleys roared to life. The man in the front shot his arm to the sky and circled. Apparently, that was the universal sign for everything. They drove away, leaving us on the side of the access road empty handed. Nothing like days of planning going to shit in a matter of minutes.

"Walker?" Command came through my comm.

"Go for Walker."

"You have a nine-one-one call. Go turn your cell on. You're dismissed. The rest of your team will hitch a ride home. Get your ass back to Savannah. Now."

What the fuck?

I jumped into the government issued SUV and found my personal cell phone stored in the glove box. With my heart constricting it felt like hours as I waited for it to power up.

Finally.

DAD: Lowe out on bail. Snatched Delaney. Mercy's going in.

DAD: When you get this check in.

DAD: Lowe has Mercy and Delaney.

DAD: GET YOUR ASS HOME.

DAD: No updates. Called in my team. Search and rescue underway.

DAD: Nothing yet. Call me. ASAP.

"Get out of the driver's seat," Tito barked.

"What?"

"Scoot your ass over. I'm driving."

"What?"

"Dude, I'm speaking English. No way am I letting you drive an hour home after I just heard the noise that came from this vehicle."

I hadn't realized I'd made any noises. I hadn't realized I was even breathing. It was as if all of the oxygen had been sucked out of the SUV. No, that wasn't right. The air had been stolen from my world. My sister and the woman I loved were in the hands of a man who was out for revenge.

I dialed my dad's number and waited.

"You on your way?"

"Hour out. Any updates?"

"Blake is working on locating Delaney's car. Both cell phones are off or gone."

"How long has he had them?"

I guess I could've checked the timestamps on my dad's texts, but I didn't want to read his messages again.

"An hour."

"An hour? Fuck."

Tito slammed on the gas, pushing me against the headrest. A damn hour. He could've already— No. I couldn't go there. I had to keep my shit together.

"You just get here. Safely."

"If one goddamn hair—"

"We got this, Bud. Walk in the park. Your sister is tough. And your woman was on a mission. They'll hold strong until we get there."

"Tito's already got us on the road. Where are we headed?"

"The house. If something changes, I'll call."

My dad disconnected, Tito drove, and I plotted. The motherfucker might want revenge. But I was doling out my own brand of retribution.

30

I WAS GOING to kick Derek Lowe's ass. One way or another, I was getting my licks in. I was waiting. As long as he had his gun pointed at Delaney's head there was nothing I could do but be ready when the opportunity arose. He'd driven us around the corner, stopped in a parking lot, pulled Delaney out of her car, and shoved us into his car much the same way we'd gotten into Delaney's.

Smart bastard.

He'd driven us around for a long time before pulling into a neighborhood. I couldn't understand what he was doing until he pulled into the driveway of a house that was for sale. With his gun still trained on Delaney, I walked beside her as he guided us to the back of the house. He broke the window out of a side door, reached in, unlocked it, and shoved us in.

I knew Delaney was scared, but something else seemed to be wrong. She'd kept her arms wrapped around herself and had obeyed Derek's every order. If I could've gotten her attention, there was a possibility I could've overtaken him while he was fucking with the door. But with Delaney in full-on shutdown mode there wasn't a damn thing I could do. I was too afraid she'd get hurt.

"Not so chatty now, huh, Delaney? Fucking busy-body bitch." Lowe kicked the back of her knee, forcing her leg to suddenly bend, and she pitched forward, hitting the floor. "You need to learn to keep your mouth shut."

"She didn't say anything. You got it all wrong. You were selling to teenagers. Did you really think they wouldn't blab? All it took was for us to arrest one and they turned on you," I lied. I'd lie my ass off, tell as many tall tales as I needed to in order to get Delaney to safety. "You fucked up and grabbed the wrong girl. Let her go. You have me and I'm the one you want. I'm the one that locked you up. Waltzed right into your house while you were in the shower and cuffed your ass."

He turned his gun toward me. I felt the white-hot pain sear through my shoulder before I'd registered the sound of the gun firing.

"Oh my God!" Delaney screamed.

She got to her hands and knees, trying to scrabble

away. I watched in horror as Lowe drew his leg back and kicked her stomach, the force nearly lifting her off the floor. He placed a second one to her face before I could stop him. Her head snapped back, spittle flew out of her mouth accompanied by blood, and she rolled to her side. I couldn't let him turn his gun back to me or I was dead. Even if I was damn lucky, his aim sucked. He pulled his shot the first time, I may not get so lucky the second.

"Nosey, fucking—"

I slammed into Lowe and gasped in pain as our bodies collided and we stumbled back. Wood smashed, and I fought to regain my balance. He was too big for me to wrestle on the floor. My years of training told me I had to stay upright and fight.

"Run!" I shouted to Delaney. "Get the fuck out of here."

I didn't have time to see if she'd followed my directions. Lowe held firm on his gun. My knee made contact with his groin, and my elbow to his face. His bare knuckles made contact with my cheek and pain blossomed, making me dizzy. Fists flew, knees and elbows collided. We tumbled to the carpet with a heavy thud that took my breath.

"Fucking bitch!" he shouted in my face. Blood poured from his nose onto my neck.

I struggled to get him off me, knowing that was the worst position I could have been in. He wouldn't budge. He used the grip of his gun to smack me in the face. My vision faded. I had to move. Had to get the gun out of his hands. My fingernails dug into his face, scoring the flesh as I dragged them down his cheek. If I wasn't in fear for my life, I would've been happy when rivulets of blood appeared.

He pitched to the side, trying to get away from my flaying hands. His movement was just what I needed. I bucked my hips as hard as I could, used my hands on his shoulders, and pushed with all my might. We rolled to the side. Almost. He was too big and too angry. It didn't take much for him to straddle my waist again. My hand grabbed at the gun. If I couldn't get it from him, I wanted to at least discharge the bullets into the wall. I hoped to God, Delaney had followed my instructions and had run. I didn't want her getting hit. All of his weight was sitting on my stomach, threatening to take what little oxygen I could suck in. Breathing hard from exertion, the pressure of his body was not my friend.

I finally got my finger into the trigger guard and pressed. One bullet shot into the ceiling, and the next into the wall to my right. I tried to fire again, but he was pulling away. In a move I could never again replicate, but I thanked the universe and all the saints for, I twisted his wrist and pressed the trigger again.

Blood sprayed in every direction. Bone and brain matter followed. The coppery taste in my mouth had me gagging. Lowe slumped forward and to the side, still mostly on top of me. I wasn't sure if I wanted to lay there with him draped over me and catch my breath or if I was going to vomit at the sight. My ears were ringing, and every muscle in my body was screaming in pain.

Every. Part.

But I was alive. Delaney was alive. Lowe was dead.

"Mercy!" I heard Jasper's voice and, for the first time since all of this started, I wanted to cry.

Lowe's body was pushed off mine and Jason's dad was on his knees by my side.

"I'm fine. Delaney's hurt."

"Clark, Lenox, and Levi have her. Let's get you up."

"Delaney needs a doctor. He kicked her in the head." Even in my haze I couldn't miss the murderous rage on his face. "I tried, Jasper. I couldn't stop him soon enough."

Adrenaline seeped out of my body with every exhale. Exhaustion was pulling me under. I was so damn tired all I wanted to do was close my eyes for a moment.

I heard talking and orders being barked, but the voices were drifting further and further away.

I needed to rest, just for a moment.

31

TITO APPROACHED the entrance to the hospital at a high rate of speed. In a move straight out of a Bourne thriller he came to a screeching, sliding stop in front of the emergency room doors.

My dad had called thirty minutes ago to redirect me to General Hospital. His short, clipped SITREP consisted of: GSW to Mercy's shoulder, Delaney was unconscious but breathing, Lowe was DOA. Nothing further. No details. He'd hung up before I could ask.

Mercy was shot. Delaney was hurt. And the motherfucker was lucky he was dead.

I muttered a quick thanks to Tito and took off to find a nurses' station. Before I could ask where Mercy or my sister were, my dad stepped off the elevator and called me over. We stepped into the lift and waited for the doors to slide closed before he spoke.

"Delaney's fine. She's awake, but barely talking. She even asked everyone, including your mom to step out of the room when the doctor came in to speak to her. Mercy is one floor up in surgery. Lenox and Lily are up there in the waiting room in case the doctor has news."

"What the fuck happened? How the hell did Lowe get his hands on Delaney in the first place?"

My dad explained my sister had a doctor's appointment this morning and had taken the day off work. She noticed Lowe was following her. She got scared and pulled into a parking lot with a bank. Her plan was to make a run for it and hope the bank's security guard could protect her.

"Why the hell did she get out of the car? She knows better."

"Her gas light was on. She was afraid she'd run out of gas. She figured the bank was her safest option. Only Lowe overpowered her and pushed her back into her car. That's when he texted Mercy from Delaney's phone."

Everything that could've gone wrong seemed to have.

"And Mercy didn't wait for backup?"

"Lowe gave her a five-minute clock. She was at the high school thinking Delaney was there when she texted that she needed help. There's a Detective

Adams upstairs, too. He's not too happy she didn't wait for him."

My teeth ground at the mention of Bruce's name. I bet he was up there. All *too happy* I wasn't. If the jacknut even thought he was going to be by Mercy's side, he was mistaken.

"How'd you get a lock on them? Delaney's car pan out?"

"We found her car in the bank parking lot. Cameras showed the girls getting into his car. He had a gun pointed at Delaney. It looked like Mercy was willing to do anything he asked to keep Delaney safe. She got right into the back seat without a fight. We were able to track Lowe driving aimlessly around through traffic cams, but when he pulled off the main road, we lost him. Lenox, Clark, Levi, and I drove through every neighborhood looking for his car. We got fucking lucky. Blake was monitoring police radios and a nine-one-one call came in with shots fired. We hauled ass and broke down the front door in time to watch half the fucker's face blow off."

"Who took the shot?"

"Mercy. Point blank."

My world stopped spinning. "Mercy?"

Christ. Taking a life leaves a mark on your soul, even if it was justified and necessary. But up close and personal? That fucks with your head. I needed to see her.

"How much longer until she's out?"

"Doctor said a few hours. So I'd say you have more than an hour."

The elevator doors opened, we stepped out, and my dad stopped me. "Listen." So much anguish stared back at me I braced for his next words. "The side of your sister's face is . . . not pretty. We're lucky he didn't shatter her cheek. It's bruised already and swollen pretty badly. You're gonna need to keep your shit in check. I already had to remove your aunts from the room once. Delaney does not need to see her family breaking down. She's scared shitless. Not talking. Staring off into space."

Shit. Goddamn. It took more than a few cleansing exhales to pull myself together. My baby sister. Motherfuck! Dad was a hundred percent right. My mom and aunts were all probably ready to have a come apart. I had to be strong, for all of them.

Delaney first, then Mercy. With one last breath I nodded, and my dad continued to her room and opened the door. My mom jumped up and rushed to me, I wrapped her in a hug and let her silently sob in my arms.

"She saved your sister," Mom whispered. I squeezed her tighter. "She's hurt, because she was protecting . . .” Mom's words were muffled as she shoved her face into my chest.

“Mercy's strong. She'll be fine. They both are. You'll see, Mama, everything will be fine.”

God, I hoped I was right. I felt my mom nod before she pulled away and gave me what was supposed to be a smile. But it looked like a tearful grimace instead. “Go sit with your sister a minute.”

“Where are Quinn and the twins?”

“They're on their way now.”

I glanced at my sister. She looked so small lying in the hospital bed with the blanket pulled up to her neck. She was faced away from us, and I was grateful for an extra moment to fortify my reaction.

“Hey there, DeeDee.” I used the old nickname she hated.

Her eyes came to me, but she didn't say anything. Thank fuck my dad had warned me about her face. He'd said it was swollen but he hadn't warned me her left eye was forced closed from the inflammation. There was also what looked close to being a boot sized bruise covering her face, from chin to forehead. Motherfucker kicked her square on the side of her head.

I sat down and pried her clasped hands apart, holding onto them when she tried to pull them back. She whimpered but didn't protest further.

Long seconds turned into minutes. The silence

stretched as Delaney stared off into space. Hurt and fear were the only things I could see. Finally, she squeezed my hand. She opened her mouth to speak but had to clear her throat several times before she croaked, "How's Mercy?"

"She'll be fine."

"Don't treat me with kid gloves like Mom and Dad do. How is she?"

"I don't know. I haven't seen her yet."

I was purposefully being evasive. I didn't want to tell her Mercy was in surgery if she didn't already know.

"Tell. Me!"

My sister, never leaving anything alone, would not stop until I told her. I'd stupidly hoped this one time she'd stop asking.

"She's in surgery. From what Dad said, the doctor said it would only be a few hours."

"You should go see her. I want to sleep."

Delaney was basically kicking me out of her room. She pulled her hand out of mine and closed her eyes, cutting off any further discussion.

"I love you, baby sis. We'll get through this."

My heart shattered when tears rolled down her battered cheek.

"She saved my life," Delaney whispered. "He shot her. I was frozen."

"Listen to me." She kept her eyes closed and made no effort to open them. "You did what Mercy needed you to do. Stayed down and out of the way so she could fight. I'm right, Delaney. She knew what she was doing. All she needed was you to stay safe while she did what she had to do."

I didn't move. I couldn't. I was almost paralyzed with fear. If the sight of my sister was breaking me, Mercy would bring me to my knees.

32

THE UNMISTAKABLE SMELL of antiseptic and the beeping of machines pulled me from sleep. Or was I still dreaming? I could've sworn Jason's cologne mingled with the disinfectant. If that was the case, I wanted to stay asleep. Maybe he'd show up in my nocturnal fantasyland and carry me off into the happily ever after. But that wasn't going to happen, the more awake I became, the more I remembered. Jason had left me.

Lowe had taken Delaney.

Shit, Delaney!

My eyes popped open and I searched for the damn button to call the nurse. I needed to check on Delaney.

"Easy, baby. Slow down before you rip your stitches."

Baby?

My groggy vision started to clear, and the man sitting next to my bed came into focus. Nope, not a dream. The shock of seeing Jason was nearly as painful as the gunshot wound in my shoulder.

Ignoring my heart as it thundered in my chest, I asked, "Where's your sister? Is she okay?"

"She's fine. Thanks to you. My parents are downstairs with her."

Thank God. Relief washed over me. "Her head's okay? I mean, she doesn't have a concussion?"

"No. A few bruises that will heal and a whole lotta scared. That part will take longer to get over."

Damn.

Now that my worry about Delaney's physical state was assuaged, I studied Jason. He looked horrible. Anguish and anger were clear. But there was something else lurking behind his eyes, trepidation, maybe. Whatever the look, I didn't want to examine it too closely. It was too painful being near him.

"You should go be with your family."

"No."

"No? Really, Jason, they need you with them."

"I *need* to be up here with you."

What the hell was this? Perhaps the medication I'd clearly received, because I wasn't in any pain, was causing me to hallucinate. Jason didn't want to be anywhere near me. He'd made himself more than clear. Even after I'd pleaded with him to stay.

"Just go. Please. Honestly, you being here isn't making anything better for me."

"I need to talk to you. Explain a few things."

"No, you don't. You leaving me told me everything I needed to know."

"Please, Mercy. Five minutes."

"Funny, a few weeks ago, I remember asking you for the same. I begged you to hear me out. Let *me* explain. You refused and walked out the door. Your decision. Now it's mine. I'm asking you to leave."

"I fucked up."

"You did."

"I'm gonna make it right, Mercy."

"You can't. It's too late."

He stood and stared down at me. "It's never too late. I'll fix what I broke. I don't care if I have to crawl back to you on my hands and knees. I will fix this," he promised. He leaned forward and placed his warm lips on my forehead. "I love you so damn much. There hasn't been a single night I haven't laid awake and thought about you. How badly I'd screwed up. How much I missed you. I'm coming for you, Mercy James. One way or another I'm coming."

He stood and made his way to the door. With his

hand on the knob he turned back and looked at me. There was no sadness, only determination.

———

"IF YOU ASK me if I need another pillow one more time, I'm going to smother you with one of the three you've propped up behind me," I grouched.

"Whatever. I'd like to see you try. You can't even lift your arm high enough to swat a fly."

Tuesday wasn't wrong. The pain meds were wearing off, but I knew I'd fall asleep again as soon as the nurse gave me more and I wanted to visit with my best friend. She was better medicine than the pharmaceuticals anyway. I hadn't told her about Jason's visit. I knew what she'd say. She was a big ol' softy and would tell me to hear him out. She was big on second chances. But not thirds. You had two chances with Tuesday before she tossed you out on your ass and locked the door behind you. She'd tell me that everyone screws up. Everyone says things they're ashamed of and should be given a chance to make it right. I understood her point of view—I just didn't agree.

"Thanks for being here," I told her.

"Shut up. Like I'd be anywhere else. Now scoot your wide ass over and make room for me. This chair sucks."

"I do not have a wide ass."

"Well, you must, it's taking up the whole damn bed."

Her smile broke into laughter. After the day I'd had it felt good to laugh.

———

TUESDAY HAD STAYED ALL DAY. She'd sat with me when the police came in to speak with me. When the agent in charge of my division came in and put me on mandatory administrative leave. And she'd held me while I'd cried. I knew it was procedure but it stung knowing my creds and gun would be locked up. As far as the police were concerned it was a justified shooting. The DEA would follow suit and there would be no review board. My boss and his boss would go over the reports, as was protocol when an agent discharged their weapon, but there would be no repercussions as a result of taking Derek Lowe's miserable life.

Tuesday was still hogging most of my hospital bed when a knock sounded. A glance at the clock told me it was after eleven. The nurses didn't knock. It was after visiting hours, they were making an exception for Tuesday. Surely, they wouldn't let Jason back here. Or would they? All it would take was one of his panty-melting smiles and a flash of his shield, and they'd pave the way for him.

Shit. I could feel Tuesday giving me the side-eye, wondering why I hadn't asked the person behind the door to enter.

"Come in!" I finally yelled.

The door slowly opened and Delaney poked her head in.

"Oh, I'm sorry. I didn't know you had—"

"No. Wait. Come in."

"I'll come—"

"Delaney?" Tuesday asked and stood. "Hey, I'm Tuesday. Please come in."

"I don't want to bother you guys." Delaney was still holding onto the door frame.

This was not the Delaney I knew. She'd never been shy or timid.

"Don't be silly. We were just watching TV, and Mercy was trying to kick me out."

"Yeah, because you were pushing me off my own bed." I turned back to Delaney. "Please come in."

She took a few steps into the room and stopped. Thankfully, the nurse had disconnected my IV a few hours ago leaving only a catheter in my hand, so I wouldn't need to be stuck again. Other than the itchy tape holding it in place, the hep-lock was barely noticeable. I threw my legs over the side of the bed and waited, heeding the warning about getting up too quickly. Once I felt stable, I stood and padded over to Delaney.

"You shouldn't be out of bed," she scolded.

"Neither should you. Yet here we are, two rebels."

Her face didn't budge at my attempt at a joke.

"I'm sorry," she whispered.

"For what? You didn't do anything wrong."

"I called you for help, and you got hurt."

"Come sit with me."

I didn't give her time to answer, I simply grabbed her hand and pulled her to the unmade hospital bed. The guilt she was feeling was normal, I felt it, too. I hadn't protected Delaney from Lowe the way I'd intended. She'd still been hurt, and the angry purple and green bruising on her face was proof. But I'd tried the best I could, and she'd done the right thing calling me.

"What else is wrong?" I asked.

"Everything."

"You know my shoulder will be fine. Besides I get two weeks paid vacation now." Still nothing. Damn. "Seriously, Delaney, I'm fine. It's the nature of my job. Not the first time I've been in a scuffle resulting in some black and blue marks and it won't be my last. All of this." I waved to my face then to hers. "Will be gone in a few weeks. But the emotional stuff won't be if you let it fester. You need to get it all out."

Delaney's head dropped forward and she stared at the linoleum floor.

"I'm going to go find us some junk food. I have my cell if you think of something you'd like." Tuesday being Tuesday, my kindhearted, intuitive friend, had picked up on Delaney's need to talk. And she probably wouldn't do that with her in the room.

I gave Tuesday a tight smile as she left. After a few minutes of silence, I knew Delaney wasn't going to offer any information. I'd have to pull every last detail from her.

"You didn't go to school today because you had a doctor's appointment. Is everything okay?"

"It was."

Was? We'd definitely come back to that.

"You made the right decision stopping at the bank. You couldn't chance running out of gas. That was a smart choice."

Jasper and Emily had both come to my room to try and thank me for helping Delaney. I wasn't having any of their gratitude, I'd done what I'd done because it was the right thing to do. I admit, I made certain decisions because it was Delaney and I didn't want her alone with Lowe. But I'd like to think I would've made the same plays had it been a stranger, but deep down, in my heart of hearts, I wasn't a hundred percent sure.

"I should've called nine-one-one."

"They wouldn't have gotten to you in time. And if they had, there would've been a showdown in the parking lot and Lowe would've shot you."

"So, instead he shot you. And beat you up."

"In the shoulder. It's nothing. I already told you, not the first time a bad guy has taken his desperation out on my face, won't be the last. None of this is on you. Derek Lowe was a piece of shit drug dealer. All of this is his fault."

Again, the silence stretched. Delaney picked at her oversized sweatshirt.

"What's wrong? I know you're upset I was hurt. But there's something else."

"If I tell you a secret, do you promise not to tell anyone? Not even Jason?"

Well, that was easy, I had no plans to talk to him again.

"Yes."

"My doctor's appointment today? It was with my OB." Obstetrician? Oh, shit. I reached over and grabbed Delaney's hand silently urging her to continue. "Twelve weeks. Everything was going perfectly."

Was! There was that word again.

"Does Carter know?"

I assumed the baby was Carter's. From what Jason had told me the two of them were it for each other. I couldn't see Delaney running and having a one-night stand or even a relationship with anyone else while she was in love with Carter Lenox.

"No. He's off on one of his secret missions." She laughed with no humor. "This is what we do. He sneaks home, says goodbye to me, tells me all the reasons we can't be together, then he runs off to places unknown, and I don't hear from him until he comes home. Hell, sometimes he doesn't even call to tell me he's back. He just shows up at some family gathering, and that's how I find out."

None of that sounded good.

"That's kinda fucked-up," I noted.

"Kinda? It's all kinds of screwed up. I'm fully aware our relationship isn't ideal. Shit, that's not even the right word. What I mean is, I know what I'm getting into when he comes over. I've been in love with him since I was sixteen. He was my first. My one and only. I know he loves me, God knows, he tells me enough. He's never asked me to wait for him. I just can't let him go. But maybe it's time."

"Why now?"

The tears that were brimming in her eyes finally

fell and streamed down her cheeks. "He'll never forgive me for losing his baby."

"What? No!"

All her wases made sense. Fucking Derek Lowe. I wished I could go back in time and kick him in the balls a few more times for what he'd done to Delaney.

"If I would've listened to you and Jason in the first place and not followed Derek, none of this would've happened. He wouldn't have wanted revenge."

"Delaney, you've done nothing wrong. Nothing! There's no way Carter will blame you for miscarrying."

"You're right. Because I'm never going to tell him. Carter's told me a thousand times I deserve better than him. Better than waiting around for a call telling me he's dead. I've never believed that. But *he* deserves a better woman, one that can keep his unborn child safe and—"

She couldn't finish her statement through her sobs. I wrapped my arms around her, gritting through the pain of lifting my bad arm.

"Your shoulder," she complained.

"Fuck my shoulder."

I squeezed her tighter and as the pain radiated down my arm and threatened to steal my breath, I knew the anguish she was feeling was far worse than any gunshot wound ever could be.

Fucking Derek Lowe. Damn him to hell.

I KNEW Mercy was out of the hospital. I also knew Tuesday had taken her home and was staying with her. Mercy would likely get pissed at Tuesday when she found out her friend had texted me back after the fifteen messages I'd sent. But I couldn't find it in myself to be anything other than grateful I had some line of information flowing.

Tuesday had started the conversation the way any good best friend would, she told me to fuck off. It had taken several messages explaining I knew I'd been wrong, taking responsibility, and groveling before she'd answered my questions about Mercy. The first few days when I'd asked how she was all I'd gotten back was, she's fine. After day five she gave me a little more, telling me Mercy'd gone back to the doctor and everything was healing the way it should and she'd start physical therapy in another week.

I planned on being there for those appointments. When I'd told Tuesday as much, she'd laughed, or I assumed she did by the number of laughing emojis she'd sent along with a, good luck with that, pal. I'd like to think I didn't need luck. I had unwavering love on my side, but the truth was I need it. A whole lotta luck, actually. Mercy hadn't returned any of my calls or text messages. Once I'd filled her voicemail with enough I'm sorrys to fill the pages of *War and Peace* with liberal amounts of I was so wrong thrown in, I was left with only text messages as a way to communicate. Which was fine. She never answered, but she was reading them. Every morning I made sure she knew I was thinking about her and every night I told her my dreams would be filled with her in my arms. And that was the truth. Each night, I'd dreamt of her. There were no more nightmares about her being ripped from my life or dying in my arms. My sleep was peaceful. The two of us were together. Now if I could convince her to give me a second chance, I wouldn't have to dream about it.

"Yo!" my dad called from my front door. "We're here."

"Kitchen," I answered.

"What are you doing?" my mom asked when she and my dad came around the corner.

"Packing."

"I see that. Why?"

"Sold the house." My dad's smile told me he was proud. My mom's quick inhale told me she was shocked. "I got lucky. I was talking to Tito on the drive to the hospital. I mentioned that I wanted to dump this place. Don't even remember why we were talking about it. I was a mess and he was trying to keep me occupied. Anyway, seems someone was looking out for me, because Tito's aunt and uncle wanted to move down to Georgia from Maryland but they couldn't find a place they liked in their price range. They liked the house, so I made it fit their budget. The inspection still has to go through, but they want it by the end of the month. I want to be out by this weekend."

"This weekend? That's in two days, Jason," my mom noted.

"Yep."

My dad had remained quiet, but I knew he understood. I couldn't go after Mercy while still living in what he called a "pit of gloom." It was time I unpacked my baggage before it cost me more than I was willing to pay.

"Why the rush?"

"A wise man once told me it was time to open the

curtains and let the sun shine in. I can't do that while living here. There are too many memories. Most of them are good. But the ones that are bad are crushing. It's time to move on."

Dad pulled my crying mom into his arms. She fit perfectly. After all these years and five kids later, they were still amazing together. They'd grown closer, their love was consuming, and my dad still looked at Emily Walker like she was going to be his last meal. And when my mom looked at my dad with her soft eyes and wonky smile, I knew she felt the same way. As a son, it grossed me out, as a man, there was nothing I wanted more.

Forever love.

I wanted that. By the grace of God, I'd found Mercy. Then I'd carelessly tossed the love she'd given me back in her face. All I needed was one more chance, and selling this house was the first step.

"What do you need from us, Bud."

There it was, Dad offering to do anything I needed him to do to help me.

"I'm renting a one-bedroom apartment. I don't need most of this crap anymore and I don't want a storage unit. Mom, I was thinking you may know someone who'd want the furniture in the guest room. All I'm taking is my living room and bedroom."

"Why are you renting? There are plenty—"

"Em, baby, he's not planning on staying in the apartment for long."

"Oh." My mom directed one of her bright mom smiles in my direction. "Well, yeah, there are plenty of women at the shelter who could really use whatever you wanted to give."

My mom and aunts all volunteered at a battered women's shelter. I wanted my stuff to go to them. My dad, uncles, my cousins, Ethan, Nick, Carter, Jackson, and I all taught self-defense there as well.

"Great. Maybe Uncle Levi, Uncle—"

"You know everyone will help," my dad cut me off. "When would you like them here?"

"Saturday morning?"

"We'll be here," he promised.

"I'll bring your sisters and aunts over. We can get the stuff ready for the shelter and get the house clean."

"You don't need to clean, Mama, I'll hire someone."

"No, you won't." My mom stopped to gather her emotions. "The family will do it."

Family. The people I'd shut out over the last two years.

"Thank you."

"No need to thank us, son. I'm proud of you."

"Proud? I've done nothing but screw up and push everyone away. There's nothing to be proud of."

"Son, life is all about failures and lessons. If you're

not failing, you're not dreaming big enough. If you're not messing up and letting down the people you love, then you're not living. And if you're not letting *yourself* down, you're not learning. No one's perfect. Not your dad, not you, not your sisters, and God knows I'm not. It's all about what you do with the hurt you caused. That's the sign of true remorse and growth. Are you self-aware enough to recognize your short comings and do you have the strength to own them and fix them? The great part about our family is while we all have our own lives, our own branches, we are bound together by our roots. They are solid, son, unbreakable. We've given you the foundation you need to dream and learn and fail. We expect the bumps in the road. No one ever said your path would be without potholes."

My mom was right, she always was. It'd taken me into my twenties to realize that when Emily Walker told you something, you'd better listen. If she gave you advice, it was spot on. And if my mom said our family was solid, even after I'd screwed up, then it was.

"What are these?" My dad had picked up the separation agreement off the counter before I could stop him. "Why do you still have this?"

It was bad enough telling Mercy I still had those documents and that I'd used them as a way to feed my guilt over the years. I really didn't want to tell my mom and dad.

"I actually was getting ready to throw them away."

I wasn't going to explain to him I didn't need them anymore.

He handed me the papers and I glanced down at them. The agreement was out of order, the signature page was on the top instead of the bottom. I stared at Kayla's pretty script and thought it was much like her. Sweet, flowy, and innocent. Nothing like the fiery woman Mercy was. I waited for the normal guilt to hit at comparing the two women, but it was absent. I wasn't comparing, I was merely making an observation. With my hands on the top of the papers I ripped them down the middle. Turning them, I ripped them again into fourths.

That was it.

I opened the lid of the trash can and threw them away. No anxiety, no trepidation, no fanfare. Nothing. Not even relief or a sense of a weight being lifted from my shoulders. I didn't feel a goddamn thing about throwing away the separation agreement. And, if I was being honest, it was kind of annoying. I'd thought there'd be something. Anything. Not the utter indifference I was feeling.

"There's nothing to feel, Bud."

"Huh?" Had I said something out loud?

"Bud, your confusion is written clear as day all over your face. You feel nothing, because there is nothing to feel. You started the process, did the work, and you already know everything you needed to know about your marriage to Kayla. Those papers you just threw away are meaningless. They don't tell your story. The relationship you had with Kayla could never have been transcribed onto paper. You know what she meant to you, and you've always known what you meant to her."

"Yeah, I guess you're right. I just thought—"

"We know what you thought, son. The friendship you had with her will always be with you. And it should. But the rest? It's in the past. And you can't move forward if you're stuck rehashing old shit."

My dad chuckled like he always did when Mom cursed. It wasn't often she did, but when she did, especially when she dropped an F-bomb the house came to a standstill.

"Have anything for us to do for you today?" Mom asked.

"No, I just wanted to talk." Mom smiled and I vowed this would be the last time I saw tears in her eyes because of me. "Thanks for coming over."

"How's Mercy?"

"Tuesday says she's doing okay. Her doctor's appointment went well."

"Any word from her?"

"Nope." I smiled.

"She's a tough one, that's for sure. Fits right in with the rest of the women in the family."

"Damn right, she does."

"When are you planning on seeing her?"

"Sunday."

"Jason, how are you going to see her if she won't even talk to you?" Mom asked.

"Really, Mom? I warned her I was coming for her. What more notice does she need?"

"Men are nuts. All of you are." She shook her head, but her smile told me I was doing the right thing.

"Perfect timing. Barbeque at Nick and Meadow's in two weeks. They have news to share. And Ethan said he and Honor have an announcement, too. Mercy will be there, right?"

"Damn right, she will be."

"Good luck, son." Mom patted my shoulder and turned to my dad. "Come on, Jasper, take me home."

"With pleasure."

"La-la-la, not in my house. Swear to—"

"Don't use the Lord's name in vain." Mom stopped me.

"Seriously. You were just telling Dad to take you home, making kissy faces at him, and you're worried about me cursing?"

"I'm a fifty-year-old woman. I don't make kissy faces."

"Like hell you don't, woman. You were making—"

"Out. Both of you. Leave. Talk about this in the car. Or outside. Pretty much anywhere but in front of me."

My dad laughed, and my mom smiled so big my heart melted.

That was what I wanted—what my parents had. And nothing was going to stop me and Mercy from having it.

34

"I'M GETTING A NEW PHONE," I announced.

"Why? You only got that one like a year ago," Tuesday questioned.

"New phone number," I corrected.

Tuesday's smirk told me she was up to something.

"Why are you smiling?"

"No reason."

"Bullshit. I know you. Spit it out."

"I just think it's amusing you're complaining the man you love is blowing up your phone when I can't even find a man I want to eat more than one meal with, let alone have sex with. And let's not even talk about men who are relationship material. There are none out there. But you? You have a great guy banging down your door and you're too stubborn to hear him out."

"He crushed me."

"He did. But do you know why?"

"Why? Whose side are you on?"

"Yours. Always yours. Especially about this. I want you to be happy. I think you need to hear him out. He knows what he did."

"What?" Tuesday's hand flew to her face and she covered her mouth. My eyes narrowed, causing her to step back. "Tuesday? What did you do? Have you been talking to him?"

"Kinda."

What the fuck? My best friend in the entire world was consorting with the enemy? How could she do this to me?

"There's no kinda. Either you are or you aren't."

"When you wouldn't answer his calls or texts, he started blowing up my phone. I ignored the first five thousand."

"Five thousand?"

"Okay, that's an exaggeration. It was more like ten or fifteen. All he wanted to know was if you were okay. That was it. I told him to fuck off, but he refused to stop pushing. Then he told me why he left. And he knows what he did was wrong and all he wants is the chance to tell you."

"So he wants me to give him the courtesy he wouldn't give me?"

"Yes."

Was she living on a different planet?

"And that's fair how?"

"It's totally not." I wanted to throw my hands up in exasperation. *Why the hell are we arguing about this if she agrees it wasn't fair.* "But, Mercy, you need to ask yourself, do you want to be right or do you want to be happy?"

"What the hell is that supposed to mean?"

"It means, Jason fucked up. He knows it, you know it, I know it, every-fucking-body knows it. So do you want to hold onto what's fair or do you want to be happy? Do you want to punish him, in turn punishing yourself, or do you want to be happy? Do you want to be as stubborn as you can be and continue to shut him out because he did it to you, or do you want to hear him out and let him fix what he broke? Because I'm telling you, that man loves you, and one day you're going to regret not hearing him out."

I should've been really pissed at my friend. She'd gone behind my back and talked to Jason. Even if it was through texts, she'd communicated with him knowing he'd broken my heart.

"Why'd you talk to him?"

"Because I knew you'd do the same for me."

"What?"

"You'd try and stop me if you thought I was making a mistake."

That was true. I would.

"So you think me shutting Jason out is a mistake?"

"An epic one."

"And if it's not? And he does it to me again. Only this time it's years from now when I'm so tangled in him I can't find my way out?"

"It won't happen."

"How can you know that, Tuesday? I talk a big game about how tough I am. Just move on. Close the boxes up nice and tight and never look back. But you know me. You know how badly I hurt. How hard it is for me. Each time I move on from something bad, it takes another bite out of my sanity."

"I know things you don't about what Jason's been doing. That's how I know. But, say you're right. Say, ten years from now he walks. Then we pick you up, dust you off, and move on. The Mercy James I know does not let fear rule her life. And that's what you're doing." Before I could speak, she continued, "Oh, and I forgot, if Jason ever screws you over, we buy a pig farm in Montana and a wood chipper."

"What do you know?" I asked, ignoring her murder plot.

"Nope. He needs to be the one to tell you."

"That's not—" My phone chirped with an incoming text, pulling me from the conversation. I dragged it out of my back pocket and checked the notification.

Jason.

It was the middle of the afternoon. Not his normal time of day to message me. I got a good morning text and a goodnight text. It was in those messages he told me how much he missed me. Little stuff about what was going on around the office. He'd even kept me up to date about Delaney. He obviously didn't know she and I spoke daily.

JASON: I was wondering if I could take you on a date Sunday?

"What does it say?"

"What? Like you don't know?" I snarked. "Sorry, that was a little bitchy. He's asking me on a date."

"A date?" Tuesday's surprise told me she had no idea about his plans.

"On Sunday."

"Are you going to answer?"

"I need to think about it."

"Fair enough. I'm running home to get my mail. Do you want anything while I'm out?"

"Ice cream?"

"Got it."

Tuesday grabbed her purse and headed for the door. I plopped down on the couch, suddenly exhausted even though I'd done exactly nothing all day. I couldn't stop thinking about what Tuesday had said. Was I being stubborn? Of course I was, but I was doing it to protect myself. My heart hurt. I never wanted to feel this way again. Though even after a few weeks, it hadn't gotten any better. Ugh!

My hands scrubbed over my healing face, and I remembered what Jason told me in the hospital. At the time I'd thought he'd had a look of determination as he left the room. What if I'd been wrong? Had it been love? What if I'd been wrong by not hearing him out? What if I was missing out on the best thing in my life? All these damn what-ifs.

Guess there was only one way to find out.

ME: Sure. What time?

35

SWEET JESUS, she texted me back.

I stared at her short and to the point message for what felt like an hour before I could get my fingers to type. I hadn't expected her to respond. I'd thought I'd have to ask her at least ten more times before she answered. Hell, I was expecting to have to go to her house and ask her in person. Now that she'd messaged me, I wasn't sure what to send back.

Thanks for answering? What, did I want to sound desperate? Was eight a.m. too early for a date? What the fuck was wrong with me? I was behaving like an idiot.

ME: Is three okay? I'll pick you up.
MERCY: Three's fine. What should I wear?
Nothing!
ME: Casual.

MERCY: See you then.

What now? Should I text back and say thank you? Tell her I miss her so damn bad I'd be counting down the hours. I needed to get a grip. Mercy made me lose my mind and act like a teenage boy going on his first car date.

ME: See ya.

My phone rang, flashing Carter's name. Great. I didn't think this call was going to go well.

"Hey, man, you stateside?"

"No. I got an urgent message from my dad to call home, but he's not answering. Thought I'd call you. He said it was about Delaney."

"Did you try her?"

"Yeah," he admitted. "Straight to voicemail."

"She ran into some trouble . . ." I told Carter all about my investigation, Delaney following Lowe, his arrest, and all the way to the bloody end.

"Please tell me you're fucking with me."

"'Fraid not."

"You're telling me this Lowe fuck took my woman and hit her?"

His woman? Jesus. The two of them were going to be the death of me.

"So, you finally pulled your head out of your ass and you're claiming my sister?"

"What?"

"You said, *my woman*. That mean you finally got your shit sorted?" My question was met with silence. "Yeah, that's what I thought. Delaney's bruises are fading. But, man, there's something broken in her, and she will not share. It can't be what she saw, because thankfully, she was unconscious when Mercy blew the fucker's head off. She's not uttering a word to anyone, the only thing she does say is she's fine."

"Fuckin' Walkers. Stubborn to the core."

"That's rich coming from you, friend. My sister has loved you her entire adult life. Yet you push her away because you're too pig-headed to take what she's offering you. I'm telling you, she needs you. If you ever loved her, you'll find a way to get your ass to her as soon as you're home."

"Man, that could be another month." If he didn't sound so defeated and miserable, I'd tell him to screw off and leave Delaney alone.

"Then we'll see you in a month. But I'm telling you, it's time. You've danced around long enough. It will kill her, but if you don't want her the way she wants you, rip the scab off and let her move on."

"She's the only woman I'll ever love. I just—" His statement was cut off by a loud shouting "Hey, I gotta run."

"Stay safe."

"Tell her . . . fuck. Just tell her I'll be there when I can."

The line went dead and I prayed to all things holy and good my cousin would be safe, wherever he was.

————

THE DRIVE to Mercy's was short but the wait had been long. Even moving all day yesterday and unpacking well into the night hadn't made the day go by any faster. We took a load to my new apartment and dropped it off before going back to the house to pick up the rest of the furniture I no longer needed and delivered it to a woman and her two children. No one had said a thing about me moving into an apartment, and when I'd gotten each of my aunts and uncles alone to apologize, they'd each waved me off and told me I was being ridiculous. Everyone except my Uncle Levi. He'd given me some pointers on how to win back Mercy. He'd reminded me of the begging he'd had to do when he'd screwed up with my Aunt Blake. Apparently, all the men in my family had pulled a bone headed move at least once in their lives, luckily all the women in my family knew how to forgive. But not before they'd cut my uncles down to size and showed them the error of their ways. I didn't need Mercy to tell me I'd screwed up, I knew I had. I only needed her to give me another chance.

Surprisingly, when I pulled into Mercy's neighborhood I wasn't as nervous as I'd thought I'd be. I couldn't wait to see her pretty face and great smile. That's if she did smile. She might give me dirty looks all night. It had been far too long since I'd laid eyes on her, and even longer since I'd had her in my arms. There wasn't a single thing I didn't miss about her. I pulled into her driveway and prayed she'd forgive me, if not today, one day soon.

I wouldn't take no for an answer. I couldn't. Nothing in my life felt right without her in it.

36

WHY HAD I *told Tuesday I didn't need her to wait around until Jason showed up?* He was knocking on the door and I was in a jam. Damn, I was stupid. Tuesday had helped me dress before she'd left, but, of course, after obsessing over my shirt I decided to change it. Getting it off was easy, all I had to do was unbutton it. The new shirt I'd picked out didn't have buttons. It was a cute tunic that went great with my jeans and boots. But now I was stuck up shit's creek with no paddle in sight.

"Come in!" I yelled from the hallway.

I heard the door open and close before Jason called out. "Hey."

"Sorry. I'm running a few minutes late. Make yourself at home."

Wait! Did I want him to make himself comfortable? This was just a date. One date to hear him out, not a rekindling. Fuck it. I didn't have time to dissect my word choices or the meaning behind them. I was currently stuck half in, half out of one of my favorite tops. Too far in to abort and take it off, not even close enough to being presentable. I was going to be really pissed if I had to cut it off to free myself.

"Take your time."

Yeah, I wasn't sure time would do me any good. I could move my arm enough to push it through the sleeve, but I'd forced it and now it hurt like a motherfucker to try and pull it back out. I was literally tangled in the fabric.

Gritting my teeth, I tried to push my arm through. Nothing. I couldn't do it.

"Oh, for fuck sakes," I mumbled.

"Are you okay?"

"Peachy."

"You don't sound peachy. Do you need any help?"

Why did his voice sound so close? Please, God, do not let him be in my room. Nope. Just standing in the doorway. Double peachy! Well, now that he'd seen me, I turned to face him.

"I'm stuck."

"I can see that."

"Well? Are you going to help me?"

"Would you like me to?" I wanted to punch him he looked so damn sexy and smug at the same time.

"Yes," I snapped.

He stepped farther into my room but left a respectable bit of distance between us. I wasn't sure if I was happy about that or if my heart broke a little more. Jason had never given me space. He was always touching me in some way. Yes, I should've been happy he was staying away. If he was closer it would muddle my brain, and I needed to think clearly.

"Would you like it on or off?"

Oh my God, this was so embarrassing.

"I don't know."

"Explain to me what's going on."

I told him how I'd gotten stuck and now it hurt too badly to move. Instead of laughing at me like I thought he would, his face was enraged.

"Are you mad . . . at me?" I asked through gritted teeth.

Not only was my shoulder on fire but my neck was starting to ache from the awkward angle it was trapped in.

"No, Mercy. I'm pissed at the circumstance. I'm pissed you're hurting. And I'm really fucking pissed at Derek Lowe." He stepped closer, gathering the hem of my shirt in his hands. "Is this the shirt you want to wear?"

"Yeah."

He gingerly bent my arm past where I could bend it myself and pulled the sleeve down. It felt like Jason was dressing a toddler. And the child was me. Once the shirt was clear of my bandages, he smoothed it down covering my stomach.

"There. Is that all right?"

"Yes, thank you."

My right hand went to my left elbow, and I held my arm close to my body, waiting for the pain to subside.

"Do you have pain pills to help with that?" He gestured to my arm.

"I do, but I'm taking Tylenol and Motrin instead."

"If you're in pain why the hell aren't you taking your meds?"

"First, I don't like the way they make me feel, and, second, I know how addictive they are."

"Mercy—"

"I'm fine. The acetaminophen and ibuprofen work enough to dull the pain. Now are we going to stand around all day discussing my choice of pain relief or are we going out?"

I could tell he was contemplating what to do with me. If he kept pushing, I wasn't going to be happy. I didn't like to be *handled*. I knew my body and I wasn't going to take anything stronger than what I was currently using.

"Are you up for it?"

"As long as it's not anything strenuous, I'll be fine." His assessing gaze turned into a smirk, and it didn't take a genius to know what he was thinking. "Like rope climbing or bungee cord jumping," I quickly added.

"No, nothing like that."

He turned and left my room. I silently followed him, grabbing my purse and turning off lights as we went. He opened the front door, and when I was clear of it, he turned and locked up the house using his key. Damn. I'd forgotten I'd given him that. Should I ask for it back? He made no offer to give it to me as we walked to his car. He helped me into the passenger side and rounded the hood. His long, powerful strides were as confident as they'd always been. What was I doing? Why was I watching the way he walked? Hell, why had I agreed to a date? I'd thought I could handle this, be close to him and not react. But it hurt worse than I thought it would to be right next to him and not touch him. Hold his hand, feel his arms around me, or his lips on mine. Why couldn't I stop thinking about how much I'd missed him? It wasn't even the sex I missed, though my body disagreed, I yearned to feel him wrapped around me at night. Talking to him. Hearing about his family. His voice in general. And I really wished I could hear his laugh.

No, this was not a good idea. Nothing about sitting next to Jason was fun. It was torture. And the longer I was in his presence the more I thought an afternoon of water boarding would be more pleasant.

"You're thinking awfully hard over there. Is your shoulder okay?"

Shit. I had to blink a few times before I noticed we were already out of my neighborhood.

"It's okay, a little sore." Letting him think my shoulder was what was bothering me was my best course of action. No good would come from him knowing the truth. Whatever the truth was at that point, I wasn't sure. "Where are we going?"

"My house."

Red alert! Red alert! Warning bells were going off. I didn't think being alone with him was all that great of a plan. But going to his house? The place he'd admitted he didn't like. The one he'd shared with Kayla—that was low. Why in the hell would he take me there?

"Aren't we going the wrong way?" Just because I'd never been to his home didn't mean I didn't know where he lived. And we were going in the wrong direction.

"No."

Great. The old Jason was back. The one I'd first met. One-word, short, clipped answers.

"Why are you mad?"

"Because I fucked up so badly with you, you're sitting over there worrying your lip, thinking of all the reasons you don't want to be in a car with me. You're nervous about going to my house and being alone with me. All of that is my fault. And I'm mad as hell at myself."

There was nothing to say to that. He was right, it was his fault, and I had been thinking those things. An awkward silence stretched until he pulled into an apartment complex.

"Where are we?"

"My house."

"This isn't your house," I noted, looking at the shitty apartment complex in front of us.

"It is now."

What the hell did that mean? He was out of the car and rounding the hood to my side before my brain could even formulate a response.

I was too busy taking in the unkempt exterior of the complex to engage in conversation. The worn brick façade had green mold in places, there was no land-scaping to speak of. Thankfully, he lived on the bottom floor, because the stairs in front of us looked like they were one more climb away from crumbling.

He opened his door and my eyes swung to him. "You can't live here. This place is a shithole." Jason chuckled but didn't comment as he ushered me into the apartment. "You have money trouble?"

I knew how much money Jason made. We both worked for the federal government, our salaries were based on the Federal Wage System. With his time at the DEA he made more than me, and I could afford ten times what the rent would be for this place.

"No," he answered.

"What happened to your house?"

"Sold it."

Sold it? What the hell? How does someone sell their house that quickly? Unless he'd had it on the market while we were together and he hadn't told me. That thought bothered me.

"What?"

"I sold it. The new owners take possession at the end of the month."

I looked around the small, cramped space. His nice furniture looked obscenely out of place. There wasn't even room for a kitchen table. His couch and entertainment system took up too much of the space. A matchbox sized kitchen, with a fridge that looked half the size of a regular one, was outdated and ugly. I turned and looked through the open door to the other side of the room. A bedroom. I searched the walls for another door but there wasn't one. Guests would have to go through his bedroom to use the bathroom? What kind of shit-tastic floorplan was that?

"Was this all you had in your house?"

"Nope. I gave the rest of it away."

"Gave it away? Why?"

"Don't need it where I'm going."

Going? Oh, shit. Was he moving? Was that why I was here? Was he going to tell me he'd been trans-ferred? I could barely swallow past the lump in my throat. I'd never considered he'd leave the area. He couldn't. His family was here. I was here, dammit. He would never leave his family, but they'd been some-what strained over the last few years. Maybe this was his way of making a clean break. And we weren't together, he didn't owe me anything. If that was the case then why did I feel a little sick at the thought of not seeing him?

"Why did you sell your house?"

"Leave it to you to jump straight to the heavy stuff. Let's sit down. Would you like something to drink?"

What did that mean? Why was asking why he'd sold his house a heavy question? People bought and sold houses every day.

"No, thanks. I'm fine."

I sat on his brown, leather couch and was taken by surprise by how comfortable it was. It was the type of sofa that beckoned you to lay on it with a fluffy blanket. Much nicer than mine. Reminding me, again, that his expensive furniture didn't belong here.

"I sold the house," he started, getting comfortable next to me. "For a lot of reasons. Being with you taught me a lot of things. One was I was holding onto the house for the wrong reasons. I was using it as a way to punish myself. I was hiding behind the walls, thinking the misery it provided was what I deserved. Then I got to know you. You taught me how to live again, how to love, and when I fucked up and lost you, going back to that house felt wrong."

"Wrong?"

"All wrong. I was going back in time. When what I needed to be doing was moving forward. So I sold it."

"Just like that?"

"No. Not just like that. I'd been thinking about selling it. I knew it had to go. The only time I felt like I was really home was when I was with you, at your house with you in my arms. That place meant nothing to me. I also knew that if I didn't get rid of it, I'd lose you for good. And I'm not willing to let you go."

"Why'd you leave me?"

Jason looked like I'd slapped him, his body physically jolted at my question.

"Before I explain why, I have to tell you a few things. I've told you about my relationship with Kayla.

There is no easy way to talk to you about this so I'm just going to give it all to you and hope you understand. She was my first love. When we got married, it was good between us. There wasn't a person who met her that didn't think she was sweet and kind. And it didn't bother me she needed me to protect her soft spot. You know what happened after she got sick. Our lives shifted in every way. She didn't look at me as her husband anymore. This is what I've struggled with. What did I do wrong? My dad actually pointed something out to me. There was never any passion between us. No lust-filled spark. In all the years I was with her, even as a young man, I never looked at her and thought I'd die if I didn't have her right then and there." Jason stopped and shook his head. "That really makes me sound like a dick. I looked at her as someone I was responsible for. Someone who was to be treated with kid gloves. That realization fucked with my head. But she never felt that way about me either. Never had she looked at me like I was the man that did it for her. I've been walking around with so much guilt coiled in my stomach, it was paralyzing. But I didn't do anything wrong and neither did she. We were too young. And maybe the only good thing about it was I had a really great friend in her and she had someone who would protect her."

"I'm glad you've let that go. You needed to. And I

don't think you're a dick for feeling the way you do. You were kind and gentle with her. You stood by her when, I'm sure, she was scared to death. You did the best you could. You were a good friend to her."

"I'd like to think I did. Now that brings us to you. I noticed you the first day you transferred to Georgia. I thought you were gorgeous. But I was married. Then I worked with you and I was so impressed by the way you handled yourself, how tough you were, great instincts, wicked smart. But I was married. So I did the only thing I could do. I stayed away from you. I actively and purposefully avoided working any cases that would involve you. It was the right thing for me to do.

"I never cheated on Kayla. Never looked at a woman and thought about what it would be like to be with her. But there was something different about you, and I knew I needed to stay away. And I was right. We're explosive. You draw me in, weave yourself around my heart, and make me want to lose myself. Every time I lay eyes on you I want to wrap you up and protect you. But, at the same time, I want you next to me when I'm working a case. I trust your judgement, your abilities, and your skill to have my back. My perfect partner, both on the job and off."

"Thank you."

It meant the world to me he trusted me as an agent. It was important to me he viewed me as an equal.

"But when we're home, and you catch fire, there's no containing the passion I feel for you. And I'm not comparing here, but I realized that was what was missing before. The absolute need I have for you. It's killing me being this close to you and not being allowed to touch you, to kiss you, to lay you back and feel you wrapped around me. It's lust and desire and love and necessity all rolled together. It's overwhelming and powerful. I love you so damn much it hurts. Physical, aching pain that I can't begin to describe." I didn't need him to. I felt the exact same thing he was feeling. "So when I came into the bathroom and saw you giving yourself an injection, I lost my mind. I couldn't hear anything you were saying because I was already so deep in my head, your voice was muffled. All I could think about was if I ever lost you, I'd give up. I wouldn't be able to move on."

"So you left me? That doesn't make sense. You were afraid of losing me but you threw away everything we had."

"There's more than one way to lose someone, Mercy. Losing you to a sickness would be crippling. But what if you lost that spark in your eyes, or the passion, or your need for me? What if all of it went away, and all you saw when you looked at me was a *friend*?" He spat out the word like it tasted dirty. "What if I lost that part of you? In that moment my head was so fucked-up I couldn't think straight. I couldn't tell you my fears. I couldn't tell you I was so scared all I wanted to do was run away like a coward because if you ever stopped loving me the way I love you it would kill me."

"You hurt me, Jason," I admitted.

I understood why he'd left. I think I'd known all along why he'd run out. It wasn't that hard to figure out why he'd freaked when he thought I was sick. But it was the way he'd handled it. He walked out on me. If he'd stayed and told me everything he'd just told me, we would've been fine. Now I was left with distrust. Would he do it to me again? That was the million-dollar question.

"I know I did. I'm so fucking sorry. And I know I'm asking a lot but I'd like the chance to prove to you it will never happen again."

"I don't know. What happens the next time you freak out?"

"I won't ever leave you again. I swear."

"But if you get freaked—"

"I will *not* ever leave you again."

I couldn't believe I was considering this. But what was my alternative? Tuesday was right, I'd always regret not giving him a second chance. I'd be living half a life. All because I was too afraid to let him in.

"Where are your separation papers?"

I loved Jason and wanted to be with him, but I wasn't stupid. If we were going to give this another shot, I needed to know a few things.

"Ripped them up and threw them away."

Wow. I was actually surprised. I figured he'd have to work up to letting certain things go. His separation agreement was the one I'd thought he'd have the most trouble with. He'd used those documents as a way to inflict pain on himself for a long time.

"I want kids, Jason."

"So do I."

"And if I want to continue working after we have them?"

"Then you'd work."

"And if I wanted to quit and stay home with them?"

"Then I'd be thrilled as hell you were staying home."

"If I wanted you to quit and take care of the kids?"

"I'd quit. Go to work at my dad's company and take the kids to work with me there."

"You can't take kids to work with you."

"My dad and uncles own the company. I could do anything I wanted. And you're forgetting our kids would be his grandkids. He'd be pissed if they didn't go to work with me."

I was trying to think up more questions to ask him

that would freak him out, kids and marriage were normally the big ones. He was fine with kids.

"You know, I have to give myself an injection once a month."

"I know." I was deep in thought when he reached over and took both my hands in his. "I love you so much. I promise you I will never hurt you again." He slipped off the couch and was on his knees in front of me. "I'm begging you for a second chance. Your rules. We'll go as slow as you need or we can pick up where we left off. As long as you're in my life."

"I love you, too," I whispered.

Decision made. I was getting ready to send up a silent prayer that I was making the right choice when it hit me. I didn't have to pray, I already knew. I believed Jason wouldn't run again. He'd given me what I needed—him. His truth, completely unguarded.

I glanced around his shithole apartment one more time and smiled. "Why'd you move into this dump?"

"Because I knew I wouldn't be here long." Yep. Just what I'd thought.

"And if I didn't agree to give you a second chance?"

"Wait. You said agree. You forgive me?" His smile nearly took my breath away. This was not one of his normal panty-soakers. This smile was full of boyish marvel. Which made me wonder if our sons would have that same smile.

"I do. But I'm begging you never to hurt me like that again. I'm strong, Jason. I can handle a lot, but the one thing I cannot is losing you. I've been in misery."

"I'm going to make up for every second you hurt."

"Good. I'm counting on it. You ready to go home? I'm afraid your nice couch is going to soak up the stink of this place."

"Yeah, baby, I'm ready to go home." He stood and pulled me up by my good hand. Inches separated us. "I'm gonna kiss you."

Our lips touched, and I was lost.

EPILOGUE

I COULD FINALLY BREATHE.

Even though Mercy had forgiven me, and invited me back into her life, I'd still been on edge. A week had passed of me babying Mercy and walking on eggshells, before she tossed a pillow at my head and told me to knock it off.

Tuesday was a regular at our house. I fucking loved that—ours. My dad and uncles had helped me move my couch in and Mercy's out. When she found out I didn't have any furniture in the bedroom, a last minute decision I'd made the day I'd moved out of my house, she shook her head and called me cocky. She was wrong. I hadn't been cocky, I'd been hopeful. I was willing to do anything I needed to get back into her good graces. There was no other option. Mercy was it for me.

Mercy's cell phone rang, I snagged it off the counter, expecting it to be Tuesday. She was coming with us today to the barbeque Nick and Meadow were hosting at their house. I was surprised when I saw Delaney's name on the screen.

"Hey, sis," I answered.

"Hi. Um. Is Mercy around?"

"She's in the shower."

"Oh."

Delaney had been acting off since everything went down with Lowe. But she still refused to talk to anyone about what was going on with her.

"Everything okay?"

"Yeah. Everything's fine."

"Bullshit. I was the king of fine when I was anything but. Please tell me what's going on."

"Really, Jason. I'm okay." Her voice softened. She was trying to be reassuring, but the sadness couldn't be masked.

"I love you, little sis. I know you're hurting. I may not know why, but I can hear it. I wish you'd talk to me."

"I can't. I have to get through this on my own. Just give me some time."

That was the first time she'd admitted something was wrong. It was a start. I wanted to push and demand she tell me. But it wouldn't do any good.

"I can do that. As long as you know you can tell me anything. I'll do whatever you need me to do to help you."

"I know," she sighed. "I'll see you at the barbeque."

"Do you have a message for Mercy?"

"No. I wanted to see if Tuesday was coming."

That was a lie, but I wouldn't call her out on it. "Yeah. She should be here soon. We're driving over together."

"Okay. See ya."

Delaney's haste to end the call confirmed she was lying about her reasons for wanting to talk to Mercy. I knew they talked frequently but I never asked what they spoke about, and Mercy never offered. I trusted she was helping my sister any way she could. At least she was talking to someone. Even if I wished that someone was me.

"Did I hear my phone? Is Tuesday trying to bail?" Mercy called from the bedroom.

I entered the room in time to see her drop the towel and pick up her lotion.

"Here, let me." I took the bottle out of her hand and squeezed a liberal amount into mine. Flowers and mint. A smell I loved, but liked it even more when it was on Mercy.

I knelt in front of her, starting at her ankles I massaged the cream into her skin. Working my way up to her calves, her knees, her thighs. So damn soft. I alternated between rubbing both legs at once to using both my hands on one extremity to knead her muscles. I placed a few soft kisses over her close-trimmed pubic hair, and licked over her clit for good measure before I grabbed the bottle again.

"You're such a tease," she complained.

I worked more lotion over her stomach, up to her perfect breasts. Taking one pink tip into my mouth I plumped and squeezed her perky mound before moving to the next.

"You taste so good."

"You're killing me, Jason," she moaned. "I think I'm—"

My mouth came down on hers cutting off the rest of what she was going to say. Our tongues mingled, and I prayed there'd never be another day that went by I didn't get to kiss her. I lived for this connection. Missed it when I was at work and looked forward to having it again when I was on my way home. With lotion covered hands I finished manipulating her tits and moved to her ass. My second favorite part on her body. I worked the rest of the lotion into her flesh there and when I broke the kiss she was panting.

"I'll take care of you when we get home tonight."

"Promise?"

I stopped myself from answering and thought

about my response. I would never make a promise to Mercy I couldn't keep. And I wasn't sure if I was ready to make love to her yet. Not because I didn't want to, but her shoulder was still healing, and I didn't want to hurt her.

"I promise I'll take care of you," I finally answered.

Her eyes narrowed. "Nope. I want details. How do you plan on relieving the ache you've created?"

I nuzzled her neck and kissed the soft skin there before I sucked her earlobe into my mouth. Letting go I answered, "I plan on lying you on the bed, spreading your sexy thighs nice and wide before I eat your pussy until you're screaming your orgasm."

"Mmm. That sounds good. What else?"

She was insatiable, and I loved it. She'd let me suck and lick and torture her body for as long as I liked. If I was providing orgasms, she was generously offering her flesh.

"I'll give you as many as you want."

"I want you. Not your tongue, not your fingers. I want you inside of me tonight."

"I don't want to hurt you," I reminded her.

"And I want you to trust me that if I didn't think I was ready I'd tell you."

"I do trust you. I don't trust myself. I can't control my need for you. Something in me snaps when I know you're ready to accept me into your body. It's this primal mating call that takes over, and all I want to do is consume you, push you as far as you'll let me. I want to own you. I'm not satisfied until you're a shaking, screaming mess of passion that's ready to explode."

My hands flexed, and my fingertips dug into her firm backside.

"Please, Jason. You won't hurt me."

"Anyone home?" Saved by Tuesday's loud shout.

"Shit. Close the door," Mercy whispered.

I was across the room in two strides. "We'll be right out," I called back.

"Oh, goody. I'll just wait out here while you guys play hide the sausage."

"Please tell me she didn't just say that," Mercy groaned.

"I don't see why you have a problem with it. She didn't refer to *your* dick as a sausage."

Mercy's giggle turned into an out-and-out belly laugh. Naked, standing in the middle of our room, she shook with laughter. Life didn't get much better than that.

———

"YOU SURE YOUR family doesn't care I'm crashing their party?" Tuesday asked.

"No. The more the merrier."

"You haven't met everyone have you, Mercy?"

"Not everyone. Just Jason's immediate family and his uncles," she answered, reminding me that after she'd kicked me out of her hospital room my dad and uncles had gone to check on her.

Mercy was a hero in their eyes. She'd saved Delaney's life. Mercy hadn't read the after-action reports and Delaney would never know, but Derek Lowe had enough GHL on his person to kill them both. The police had also found a batch of tablets in the trunk of his car, along with rope, duct tape, and an ax. No one will ever know for sure what his intention was, but it was safe to assume he'd planned on ending Delaney's life.

We pulled in front of Nick and Meadow's house and an old familiar feeling of happiness slid into place. It felt good having Mercy by my side. I couldn't wait to introduce her to everyone.

"Anything I should know before we go in?" Mercy asked.

"Like what?"

"I don't know. Anything. I don't want to put my foot in my mouth and have everyone hate me."

"Nothing you could say would make my family hate you."

"If you say so."

We made our way to the door, I opened it, and had to stop.

"Do you hear that?"

Loud laughter rang out through the house.

"Um?"

"I'd forgotten. But thank God, you reminded me."

Family.

"What are you talking about?"

Before I could explain, Carson ran to the front door, skidded to a stop, and put her hands on her little hips.

"There you are, Uncle Jason. Mom said I had to wait until you got here with your girlfriend to eat a cupcake. You're like five hours late." The little girl looked at Mercy, then Tuesday. "You brought two girl-friends? Is that allowed?"

"Squirt!"

"What, Daddy? Uncle Jason brought two girls. I'm just asking." Carson said to her dad, Ethan.

Tuesday chuckled and Mercy busted into a belly laugh that had her bending forward.

"I hope that one is your girlfriend, she is pretty and silly." Carson pointed to Mercy.

"Hey! I can be silly, too," Tuesday said.

"Oh my God. I love her." Mercy stepped forward and greeted her, "Hi, I'm Mercy. Your Uncle Jason's girlfriend. That is my friend, Tuesday."

"You have a cool name, like my mom. Her name is Honor," Carson beamed.

"Why, thank you very much. I like your name, too."

"Now that we've established my daughter likes your name, I'm Ethan. Nice to meet you."

"Hi, Ethan."

My mom came over and started to pull Mercy away but before she could get very far, I tugged her back to me and palmed her face, bringing it mere inches from mine. "The sound? Family. That's what all this noise is, love and family. Thank you for giving it back to me."

"Family. I like that. I never really had one."

"Now you do. They're all yours. Your new aunts and uncles, cousins, cute niece, sisters, and the best set of parents you could ever need."

"You're pretty lucky to have all of them."

"I am. We are."

I placed a chaste kiss on her lips and then let my mom drag her and Tuesday away. Never ending introductions were made over the next twenty minutes. The whole family minus my youngest sisters and Carter were there. I watched Delaney mingle and talk to everyone. She had her fake smile firmly in place, and I wondered if anyone else noticed. My eyes locked with my dad's, and his jaw clenched. Yep. He saw it, too.

Dad had given me two years before he'd had enough and sat me down for a come-to-Jesus talk. He wouldn't wait that long to set his baby girl straight. I hoped she was getting what she needed from Mercy.

Nick had asked everyone to come into the living room for their surprise announcement. I hoped they were going to announce they were finally going to adopt. Nick's wife, Meadow, had been attacked by a vicious serial killer. She narrowly escaped, but the attack left her unable to have children. They talked about it a few years back, changed their minds, thought about a surrogate, and recently I'd heard they were considering adoption again. My fingers were crossed they'd come to a definite decision.

Meadow walked down the hall, and Nick asked for everyone's attention.

"Thanks for coming. Not that we need an excuse to get together, but, today, Meadow and I want to share our good news with you. First, we've been keeping secrets from all of you. And we lied. Last weekend we did not go up to New York for a weekend getaway. We . . . um . . . shit, sorry." Nick swiped his face and everyone looked worried. "We went to California to be there for the birth of our babies," he choked and wiped another tear.

Holy shit. Did he say birth of his babies? Meadow walked back into the living room holding a tiny bundle in each arm. I don't think there was any oxygen left in the room after the collective gasp.

"We want you to meet our daughter, Ariana, and our son, Nolan."

No one moved. No one said a word. Nothing but silence until my Aunt Reagan's sob cut through the quiet. I thought I heard my Uncle Clark clear his throat and sniff a few times, too.

"Sorry we didn't tell you before. But we wanted to make sure the adoption went through and the birth mother didn't change her mind at the last minute," Meadow said. "We hope none of you are mad."

"Mad?" My Aunt Reagan asked. "We couldn't be happier for you."

"YAY! More cousins!" Carson shouted and danced around, cutting the silence.

She pulled off the sweatshirt she was wearing, and Honor tried to get to her before she got it off, but it was too late. Everyone was watching the cute little girl running around in her excitement, therefore, not missing her neon pink shirt with big white letters across the front.

BIG SISTER

"What?" My Aunt Lily gasped. "Are you—"

"Surprise," Ethan muttered.

The room broke out in excited cheers, and I wrapped my arms around Mercy.

"Never a dull moment around here. Soon there will be a whole new generation of kids invading."

"Huh?" she mumbled, and I followed her distracted gaze across the room. Jackson and Tuesday were talking. Nothing unusual there. He was probably hitting on her. Then my eyes landed on my sister. She didn't look happy. She looked devastated. Shit. I looked around and caught sight of my dad. He saw it, too. Double shit.

"I need to go talk to Delaney," Mercy mumbled.

Before she could walk away, the front door opened. "What are we celebrating?" Carter asked.

"Is that Carter?" Mercy whispered.

"Yeah."

"Fuck. I have to go get Delaney."

"What's wrong?"

"Please trust me. I love you, and if I don't come back, I'll meet you at home. She needs me right now."

"Okay. I love you, too. Go."

"Uncle Carter." Carson bounced to her uncle. "There's so much you missed. Uncle Nick and Aunt Meadow have two babies. And I'm going to be a big sister."

"Is that right? I'm a new uncle three times over." He picked Carson up and spun her around in circles. "Let me say hi to everyone and then I'll show you what I brought back for you."

"New coins?"

"You know it."

Carson ran off, not wanting to miss another moment of the celebration.

"Where's Delaney?"

"She took off."

"Fuck. I tried to get here sooner. But shit went sideways and my team had to stay."

"Hey, bro. Welcome home." Ethan came over, cutting off any further conversation.

"New kid, huh? Congratulations."

The brothers embraced and clapped each other on the back.

"I'm gonna talk to Nick." I excused myself.

There was happiness all around me, but all I could think about was my sister.

"Mercy go with her?" my dad asked before I could get through the crowd of family members now hogging the babies.

"Yeah. Didn't tell me what was wrong, just that she was leaving with Delaney and she'd meet me at home later."

"Good. Mercy will take care of her."

"What?" I eyed my dad. Was he seriously trusting Mercy with his baby girl? No one fucked with the Walker girls. And no one protected and comforted them like my dad did. Not even me. And he was handing over care to Mercy. That was huge.

"I trust Mercy. The two of them have a bond. I don't know what went down with Lowe while they were alone with him in that house. But whatever it was cemented a deep friendship. Mercy won't let her fall."

"No. She won't."

"She's your forever love, Bud. Hold on to her with both hands and never let go."

"Thanks for everything. My head was jacked. It's not anymore. I know exactly who she is and as soon as I can, I'm getting my ring on her finger."

"We got you, Bud. Always."

TWO WEEKS LATER...

Jackson Clark

"YO, JACKSON, YOU KNOW THAT WOMAN?" Brice asked.

I stopped mid-step and looked around. Doctors, nurses, and volunteers were milling about outside the Autumn Lakes Nursing Home. The small fire that had started in the craft room was out before we'd arrived. However, being the type of facility it was, the fire inspector was inside and still not allowing the elderly occupants back in until she deemed it safe. Between the EMTs on scene and the ocean of people, I had no idea who Brice was talking about.

"Who?"

"There." He pointed off to the side of the crowd. A

woman stood next to an old woman sitting in a wheelchair.

Tuesday Knowls.

The woman who'd shot me down and had plagued my dreams ever since the family barbeque at Nick and Meadow's house a few weeks back. The last thing I should've been doing at a family party was lusting after Mercy's friend, Tuesday. But she had to be the hottest woman I'd ever had the pleasure of talking to. Not only was she beyond beautiful she was wicked funny. We'd spent most of the time talking and joking around. I couldn't remember a time I'd laughed so hard. She had a fast comeback for everything.

I'd asked her if I could take her out for a drink, and she basically patted me on my head and called me kiddo. That had never happened before. She was a few years older than me, but it wasn't as if the gap would classify her as a Mrs. Robinson.

"I take it you know her," Brice called out as I took off in Tuesday's direction.

"Tuesday?"

Her eyes raked over my turnout gear, and I couldn't miss the spark when her gaze came back to mine. The uniform. It did it every time. Normally, it was a turnoff when a woman's only interest in me was because I was a firefighter. When a woman's first question was about my uniform, I knew she was a badge bunny and lost interest. But with Tuesday, I'd take all the help I could get. Hell, I'd take her on a date wearing my yellow helmet, coat, and pants if it made her say yes.

"Hi, Jackson. Everything okay in there?"

"Yeah. The staff had the fire out with an extinguisher before we arrived. Minimal damage and nothing structural. The inspector is just being cautious."

"Good."

"Aren't you going to introduce me to your gentleman caller, dear?" the old woman asked.

"Jeez, Granny. Gentleman caller is a bit dramatic, don't you think?" Tuesday laughed. "This is Jackson Clark. Remember I told you, Mercy and Jason are back together? Jackson is Jason's cousin. Jackson, this is my grandmother, Patricia Knowls."

"Pleasure to meet you, Mrs. Knowls."

"Patricia, please. Or Patty. You may call me either, as long as you promise to call," Mrs. Knowls said as she winked.

Tuesday's eyes rolled to the heavens, and I laughed along with the older woman.

"Granny!" Tuesday admonished. Which only made Patricia's smile grow.

"What?" Patricia laughed. "At my age I don't get the chance to see many good looking men. Especially in uniform. Had I known our local fire department was full of hunks I may've started a fire myself."

"You can't say that. It's not funny."

"You'll have to excuse my granddaughter. She's a little wound up today. One little fire and she's ready to break me out of this place."

"You could've been hurt."

The older woman took Tuesday's hand in hers and patted it. "I was never in any danger. Like Jackson explained. The staff had it out in minutes."

"It was nice seeing you, Jackson. We should let you get back to work."

I was being dismissed. Any other time, I call her out on it. But she obviously loved her grandmother and was more than a little worried about her safety. I'd give her this play, but her time had officially run out. I eyed the two women; the family resemblance was uncanny. I bet Patricia had been stunning when she was Tuesday's age. And besides, she was right, I did have to get back to work, though I didn't want to leave.

"Yeah. It was nice seeing you, too, Tuesday. Patty, it was a pleasure, glad you're safe."

"Hope to see you soon, young man."

"Granny!" Tuesday muttered under her breath.

I wasn't sure when I'd see Patty again, but I was going to find a way to see Tuesday. Sooner rather than later.

Jackson and Tuesday are next in Claiming Tuesday

Riley Edwards

www.RileyEdwardsRomance.com

Takeback

Dangerous Love

Dangerous Rescue

Dangerous Games

Dangerous Encounter

Dangerous Mind

Gemini Group

Nixon's Promise

Jameson's Salvation

Weston's Treasure

Alec's Dream

Chasin's Surrender

Holden's Resurrection

Jonny's Redemption

Red Team - Susan Stoker Universe

Nightstalker

Protecting Olivia

Redeeming Violet

Recovering Ivy

Rescuing Erin

The Gold Team - Susan Stoker Universe

Brooks

Thaddeus

Kyle

Maximus

Declan

Blue Team - Susan Stoker Universe

Owen

Gabe

Myles

Kevin

Cooper

Garrett

The 707 Freedom Series

Free

Freeing Jasper

Finally Free

Freedom

The Next Generation (707 spinoff)

Saving Meadow

Chasing Honor

Finding Mercy

Claiming Tuesday

Adoring Delaney

Keeping Quinn

Taking Liberty

Triple Canopy

Damaged

Flawed

Imperfect

Tarnished

Tainted

Conquered

Shattered

Fractured

The Collective

Unbroken

Trust

Standalones

Romancing Rayne

Falling for the Delta Co-written with Susan Stoker

AUDIO

Are you an Audio Fan?

Check out Riley's titles in Audio on Audible and iTunes

Gemini Group

Narrated by: Joe Arden and Erin Mallon

Red Team

Narrated by: Jason Clarke and Carly Robins

Gold Team

Narrated by: Lee Samuels and Maxine Mitchell

The 707 Series

Narrated by: Troy Duran and C. J. Bloom

The Next Generation

Narrated by: Troy Duran and Devon Grace

Triple Canopy

Narrated by: MacKenzie Cartwright and Connor Crais

More audio coming soon!

BE A REBEL

Riley Edwards is a USA Today and WSJ bestselling author, wife, and military mom. Riley was born and raised in Los Angeles but now resides on the east coast with her fantastic husband and children.

Riley writes heart-stopping romance with sexy alpha heroes and even stronger heroines. Riley's favorite genres to write are romantic suspense and military romance.

Don't forget to sign up for Riley's newsletter and never miss another release, sale, or exclusive bonus material.

Rebels Newsletter

Facebook Fan Group

www.rileyedwardsromance.com

facebook.com/Novelist.Riley.Edwards

instagram.com/rileyedwardsromance

bookbub.com/authors/riley-edwards

amazon.com/author/rileyedwards

www.ingramcontent.com/pod-product-compliance
Lightning Source LLC
Chambersburg PA
CBHW071206210726
48293CB00002B/310